re saying
ligh:

"[...] [...] uldn't wait to start the next one [...] me do that before."
—*Terrance W.*

"The suspense got to be so great I could feel the blood pounding in my ears."
—*Yolanda E.*

"Once I started reading them, I just couldn't stop, not even to go to sleep."
—*Brian M.*

"Great books! I hope they write more."
—*Eric J.*

"When I finished these books, I went back to the beginning and read them all over again. That's how much I loved them."
—*Caren B.*

"I found it very easy to lose myself in these books. They kept my interest from beginning to end and were always realistic. The characters are vivid, and the endings left me in eager anticipation of the next book."
—*Keziah J.*

BLUFORD HIGH

Someone to Love Me

ANNE SCHRAFF

Series Editor: Paul Langan

SCHOLASTIC INC.
New York Toronto London Auckland Sydney
Mexico City New Delhi Hong Kong Buenos Aires

No part of this publication may be reproduced,
stored in a retrieval system, or transmitted in any form
or by any means, electronic, mechanical, photocopying,
recording, or otherwise, without written permission of the publisher.
For information regarding permission, write to Townsend Press, Inc.,
1038 Industrial Drive, West Berlin, NJ 08091.
Visit Townsend Press on the Web at
www.townsendpress.com.

ISBN-13: 978-0-439-90486-5
ISBN-10: 0-439-90486-2

Copyright © 2002 by Townsend Press, Inc.
All rights reserved. Published by Scholastic Inc.,
557 Broadway, New York, NY 10012, by arrangement
with Townsend Press, Inc. SCHOLASTIC and associated logos
are trademarks and/or registered trademarks of Scholastic Inc.

12 11 10 9 8   10 11 12/0

Printed in the U.S.A.   01

First Scholastic printing, January 2007

Chapter 1

Cindy Gibson tripped over a stack of magazines in the middle of the living room, bumped her knee against the sharp corner of the coffee table, and dropped a can of cat food on the floor.

"Ouch, my leg!" she howled. "This place is a freakin' mess!" Her two cats, Theo and Cleo, scurried beneath the table.

Lorraine, Cindy's mother, came out of her bedroom carrying a small mirror. She peered at her reflection as she walked, carefully examining the lipstick she had just put on. "Stop whinin', baby. Just straighten things up before you leave for school. I'm late for work."

"I'm not going to school today," Cindy declared. She waited to see if her mother would get angry and insist that she go. Cindy was a freshman at Bluford High, and even though it was only

October, she had already missed several days of school.

"You better go to school, baby," her mother said, touching up her eye make-up. "If you drop out at your age, you'll end up like me, in your thirties waitin' tables at some grease pit for next to nothing. This ain't the kinda life you wanna have, girl. Believe me on that. By the way, if Raffie calls, tell him I'm off work at five tonight. Bye, baby." Cindy heard a thud as her mother closed the front door of their small apartment.

Theo, a jet-black cat, crept warily from under the table, followed by Cleo, who was gray and white. Dust and crumbs from under the table stuck delicately to each cat's coat.

Cindy brushed the cats' fur, cleaned up the spilled food, and walked out to the kitchen. Theo and Cleo followed quickly behind her. "Mom doesn't really care if I go to school," Cindy pouted, grabbing a fresh can of cat food. "All she cares about is Raffie and whether or not she's put the right gunk on her face, right, Theo?" The cat blinked and rubbed its furry face against her leg.

Theo and Cleo were Cindy's best friends. She told them everything. They were there for her whenever she was lonely or needed someone to talk to. It was more than she could say for Mom, Cindy thought.

"I ain't goin' anywhere today, Cleo. I'm stayin' right here and watchin' trashy talk shows all day. I don't care what Mom says," Cindy said, spooning chunks of cat food into Theo's and Cleo's plastic bowls.

Just then the doorbell rang. "Who is it?" Cindy cried, walking towards the door.

"It's me. Open up," a familiar voice said.

Cindy opened the door to find Jamee Wills, another Bluford freshman, staring at her.

"Cindy!" Jamee shouted. "Girl, what're you doing in pajamas? It's time to go to school."

"I'm not going to school," Cindy said firmly. "Why don't you cut too? We can watch TV, and I got popcorn we can stick in the microwave. And there's pizza in the freezer, too. Today on Paula Poole's show—"

"Cindy! Girl, get it together!" Jamee said, stepping into the apartment. "You need to throw on some clothes and come to school. Keep this up, you gonna be so

3

far behind that you can't do nothin' but fail."

"You don't understand—" Cindy replied, looking down at the worn flip-flops on her feet.

"I understand all right. I understand you gotta get back on track," Jamee replied. "Remember in middle school, Mr. Schuman said you were such a good artist you could be a famous cartoonist for Disney or something? How you gonna be famous if you don't go to school?"

Cindy shrugged. "I can't hang around school all day, Jamee. I get bored. Who cares anyway? My mom wouldn't mind if I quit school. We all just wasting our time in school anyway. Ain't none of us goin' anywhere."

"Cindy, you're crazy," Jamee said, tugging on Cindy's arm. "My sister, Darcy, she's already planning to go to college, and so is her friend Tarah. I'm gonna do the same thing, and you can do it too. But first you gotta get up, change them clothes and get to school. Now come on!"

"Just leave me alone," Cindy insisted.

"Cindy, please come to school."

"Jamee, cut school with me today," Cindy moaned. "If you don't wanna

4

watch TV, I got some CD's we could play and—"

"I'm outta here," Jamee snapped. "I'm not gonna sit here and watch you throw your life away!" Jamee stormed towards the doorway. "When you want to do something with yourself besides sit here watching TV, call me," she said, walking out the door and slamming it behind her. The loud crash of the door was followed by a heavy silence.

Cindy moved to the window and watched Jamee shift her backpack and join the stream of kids heading for Bluford. Part of her wanted to join the crowd and head to school, but another part of her did not want to move. Unlike Jamee and her classmates, Cindy felt foreign and out of place at school. Her teachers often said she was "quiet" and "shy," but Cindy knew she was just different.

Turning from the window, Cindy grabbed the magazines on the living room floor and stacked them neatly on the coffee table. Then she picked up a pile of dirty clothes she had left sitting on the living room chair for weeks.

"Yuck, these stink!" Cindy groaned. It had been a while since she had washed her laundry. Sometimes she just picked an outfit from the dirty clothes pile to wear to school. As long as things were not too dirty or wrinkled, she would still wear them. It had not always been this way. In fact, Cindy did have a few new clothes that she got for the start of her freshman year. But as weeks passed and her mother spent less and less time at home, laundry, like school, seemed less important.

Glancing around the cluttered living room, Cindy focused on the small picture of her mother that sat next to the TV. Raffie, her mother's boyfriend, was also in the picture, his arm resting on her shoulder like a heavy snake. Only a few months old, the picture captured her mother's flawless milk-chocolate skin and her radiant smile. *Mom is beautiful,* Cindy thought, *and I look nothing like her.* Where her mother was tall, curvy, and attractive, Cindy was long and skinny. But worse than her lanky shape was her nose. To Cindy, it seemed to spread too far across the middle of her face, making her feel that her head was just a platform on which her nose rested.

Friends of her mother had always been kind, but even they noticed how different Cindy was. *"Oh, I can't see a resemblance,"* they would politely begin. *"You must take after your father."* Cindy knew exactly what they were trying to say, but she appreciated their attempt to spare her feelings.

The only person who did not seem concerned with Cindy's feelings was Raffie. *"Are you sure she's your momma?"* he asked Cindy when he began dating her mother last year. When Cindy first met him, he was sitting at the kitchen table, gold chains jangling around his neck, gold earrings glittering from his earlobes, and a smirk on his face.

"You ain't nothin' like your momma," he had said. *"She is what a man would call one hot lady."* Since then, Cindy did her best to ignore Raffie, but it was not easy. Often he said things that made her feel even worse about her looks, but he always did it out of Mom's earshot, calling Cindy "Ugly Mugly" and flaring his nostrils to taunt her. Whenever Cindy asked him to stop, he would laugh in her face. Once, he even flapped his arms in a mock imitation of her long, awkward limbs.

In August, Cindy's mother announced that she and Raffie were "serious," and since then, she spent most of her free time with him. In the rare moments Mom was home, all she could talk about was Raffie. Cindy cringed each time she heard his name. It seemed to her that Raffie was gradually taking over her mother's life. Worse, it appeared as if that was exactly what Mom wanted.

Alone in the apartment, Cindy sat in the recliner in front of the TV and turned it on with the remote control. She had to push hard to make the recliner go back into a comfortable position. The old chair did not work as well as it used to, and Mom said she did not make enough money at her waitressing job to buy a new one.

Cindy had believed her until she noticed her mother frequently buying herself new outfits to wear for Raffie. It seemed that once a week Mom came home carrying shopping bags from expensive department stores. When Cindy asked her about it, Mom explained that Raffie had been giving her money so she could buy nice clothes, but this only made Cindy more upset. It was as if Raffie was buying her mother away from her, and there was nothing Cindy could do to stop it.

Cindy began flipping through the channels when she heard the doorbell ring. Annoyed, she turned toward the door and called out, "Yeah? Who is it?"

"Mrs. Davis, honey," came a familiar voice. Rose Davis lived at the other end of the hall. She was raising her fifteen-year-old grandson, Harold. Once, in the basement laundry room, Cindy overheard Mrs. Davis tell a neighbor that Harold's mother had died in childbirth, and his father never was in the picture.

Cindy got up and opened the door. "Hi, Mrs. Davis."

"Child, I heard the TV goin', so I figured you were home. I was worried about you. Ain't you supposed to be in school?" Mrs. Davis asked.

"Uh . . . I got cramps," Cindy lied, rubbing her hand on her stomach.

"Poor thing! I make tea that's real soothin' for that. I'll bring you some if you like," Mrs. Davis offered.

"No, thank you. I just took something. I'll feel better soon," Cindy said, smiling.

Rose Davis stared at her for a moment. Cindy braced herself for criticism about not being in school. But then the old woman began to smile. "Child, you got the prettiest eyes I ever did see," she said.

"Me?" Cindy said, stunned. "You must be thinkin' of my mom. She's got real pretty eyes with long lashes, but my eyes are—"

"I never noticed before that you got the prettiest hazel-brown eyes, Cindy," Mrs. Davis added. "Folks say the eyes are windows to the soul. They believe you can look someone right in the eye and tell what kind of person they are."

"Some boy in school says I have freak eyes," Cindy said. "Now, him and all his friends call me that whenever they see me."

Mrs. Davis grabbed hold of Cindy's shoulders and looked into her face. "Child, your eyes are beautiful, and don't you forget that. Pay no mind to what a boy says 'bout you. My grandson Harold tells me that some of them kids at your school can be downright nasty some- times. It's like I tell him—when they start talkin' that nonsense, you just stop lis- tenin'. Let 'em call you names. But it's you who's got the prettiest eyes around, not them. Remember that."

As she spoke, Mrs. Davis gently placed her hand on Cindy's cheek. "Some people need to see their own beauty before they can believe they got it," she said, smiling. Mrs. Davis waved goodbye and headed down the long hallway.

Cindy hurried to the bathroom mirror and stared into it. She stood for a long time, moving her face in close for a better look. Her mother had a mirror that magnified everything, and Cindy looked in that too. Her large hazel eyes stared back at her. *Did Mrs. Davis mean what she said, or was she being nice?* Cindy wondered.

Leaving the TV on, Cindy jumped in the shower and washed her hair. Then she gathered her dirty clothes, took them downstairs and put them in the washing machine. When the clothes were dry, she brought them back upstairs, folded them neatly and put them into her drawers. It was the first time she had done her laundry in weeks.

After putting the clothes away, Cindy found a pair of white jeans and two ribbed tank tops, one blue and the other green and yellow. *Maybe I'll go to school tomorrow wearing one of these tank tops*, she thought. Probably not, but if she felt like it in the morning, she might go. Mom would write a note explaining that she had been sick. Mom never seemed to care what excuses Cindy used to skip school. Cindy practically dictated them, always remembering to vary the made-up ailments. She used headaches until a nosy teacher started pushing her to see a doctor. Then she added cramps and fevers to her list of illnesses.

As Cindy thought about returning to school, she again recalled what Mrs. Davis said about her having "the prettiest eyes." She grabbed her mother's magnifying mirror and sat on the recliner looking into it. Cindy tried hard to see what Mrs. Davis saw.

"Maybe my eyes *are* pretty," Cindy said into the mirror.

On Paula Poole's show, two sisters who were married to the same man were screaming at each other. The show kept bleeping out the bad words flying between them, and when they started pulling each other's hair, the audience went wild. Everybody was laughing and cheering.

But Cindy did not pay much attention to the show. She kept staring in the mirror, trying out different expressions to see how they changed the look of her eyes. Maybe she wasn't that bad looking, she thought. With her hair clean and brushed, she didn't think she looked as ugly as Raffie said. And she had clearer skin than most of the other kids at school.

Suddenly the phone rang. Cindy put the mirror down and answered it.

"Hello," she said.

"Yo—who's this?" a familiar deep-throated voice replied.

"It's me," Cindy answered.

"Oh, Ugly Mugly," Raffie Whitaker said. "How come you home? You get suspended for messin' up at school again?"

"I never been suspended," Cindy corrected him sharply. "And stop calling me that."

Raffie laughed. He always chuckled when he upset Cindy. She could just imagine him on the other end of the line—smiling in satisfaction at how he managed to insult her. "C'mon, Ugly Mugly. Where's your momma?" he asked, still laughing.

"I told you to stop calling me that," Cindy demanded. She wished she could reach into the telephone and wrap the cord around his neck.

"Girl, you so ugly," Raffie went on, in between bursts of cackling laughter,

13

"when the doctor delivered you, he was wearin' a blindfold."

Cindy slammed down the phone. In about a second it rang again. She turned up the TV volume to drown out the ringing. One of the sisters on the Paula Poole show had a nail file, and she looked as if she was about to attack the other one with it. Maybe it was all an act, but the hate in the girl's face seemed real. It was the same hatred Cindy felt for Raffie.

Cindy fantasized about being on the show with Raffie Whitaker. She imagined herself grabbing the gold chains he hung around his neck and pulling them so tight his eyes bulged out.

The phone kept ringing. "I ain't gonna answer you. You can't make me." Cindy smiled because for once she had power. Raffie Whitaker was fuming somewhere, and he could not do a thing about it.

Ignoring the phone's periodic ringing, Cindy picked up the mirror again and repeated the words that Mrs. Davis had said. "Pretty eyes . . . pretty hazel eyes."

Maybe Mrs. Davis was not the only one who thought she was special. Maybe someone else would feel that way about her too one day.

Chapter 2

When Cindy's mother got home shortly after 5:30, the phone was still ringing. She rushed in to answer it, tossing her purse and keys on a nearby chair.

"Hello," Mom huffed, picking up the phone. "Oh, hey Raffie. What do you mean you've been calling all day? Cindy was right here. Cindy!" Cindy glanced up from the magazine she was leafing through. "Raffie's telling me he's been calling all day and nobody answered. Did you go somewhere?"

"I been right here except when I went down to do the wash, and oh, I took a shower and stuff," Cindy said.

"She what?" Mom cried. "Well, she's gonna be sorry she did that. Raffie honey, don't be like that. Listen to me, I've got chilled wine, and I'll make us some steaks. . . . Raffie, honey, listen . . . Raffie?"

Mom put down the phone and glared at Cindy. "You just have to make trouble, don't you? Raffie says you hung up on him. Did you do that?"

"He's a liar, Mom. He ain't nothin' but a liar," Cindy insisted.

"You tell me the truth, girl. You look me in the eye and tell me you didn't hang up the phone on him," her mother demanded.

"Okay, yeah, I did," Cindy admitted, throwing down the magazine. "But where does he get off calling me ugly all the time? You don't hear the stuff he says to me behind your back. He disses me big time, Mom. How come it's okay for him to do that?" Cindy glared at her mother, fighting to keep back tears of anger and hurt.

"Aw baby, he don't mean nothing when he talks like that. He's just playing. It's a bad habit he got from the street. Don't you know that by now? He's just like a little boy who likes to tease all the girls, that's all," her mother explained.

Cindy did not want to excuse Raffie's behavior, but her mother's words calmed her. "Well, I'm sorry I hung up on him, but he better be sorry for callin' me names too," she said.

"Come 'ere, baby," Mom said, "I've got something for you." Digging in her purse, she fished out two shiny tubes of lipstick. "I picked these up today at the drugstore, and one's for you. What do you think of this color?" Cindy took the offered lipstick and put it on.

"It's nice, Mom," she said, glancing in her mother's compact mirror. "Thanks."

Her mother smiled and gave her a hug. "Baby, there's TV dinners in the fridge. There's beef stew and oriental chicken. I'm gonna change and go out for a little while. You don't mind, do you?"

"It don't matter anyway," Cindy mumbled, shrugging her shoulders.

"What did you say?" her mother asked, turning around quickly.

"Nothing. I didn't say nothing," she lied.

Cindy was disappointed. She had hoped her mother might stay home for dinner, and then they could watch TV or rent a movie. Cindy thought they might even make popcorn after dinner and talk. It had been so long since they had spent time together. Since Mom and Raffie started dating, Cindy often spent evenings alone in the apartment. Nights were the worst. Theo and Cleo were there, but what she longed to hear most was another voice.

"Uh, why don't you ask a girlfriend over, baby?" Mom said, seeming to sense Cindy's sadness. "Maybe Jamee or Amberlynn could come over. Y'all always have fun together."

"They don't want to come over here to this messy place," Cindy said bitterly.

"Cindy, don't talk like that. Just because there's a little dust on the furniture doesn't mean we're not as good as the Willses and the Baileys. I won't be that late tonight, baby. Now come on and give me a smile."

Cindy turned away, and her mother let her go. Cindy heard her walk down the hallway to the bathroom. Soon she heard the shower turn on. After that, Mom would dress up for her date. It was the same routine as on so many other nights. All her mother ever did anymore was spend time with Raffie.

"Do I look all right, Cindy?" Mom asked, walking into the living room in a short black dress that showed off her long, shapely legs.

"Yeah, Mom," Cindy answered, pretending not to pay attention. She thought her mother looked beautiful.

She looked like Cindy knew she herself could never look, not with all the lipstick and pretty dresses in the world. "So what time you think you'll be home?" Cindy asked.

"Oh, I'm not sure. Don't wait up for me. Tomorrow's a school day, and you can't be missing any more days."

"Whatever," Cindy mumbled.

"Call Jamee. I'm sure she'll come over," Mom said, clutching her purse. Seconds later, Cindy heard the apartment door close. Her mother was gone.

Overwhelmed by the silence in the apartment, Cindy decided to call Amberlynn.

"Amberlynn, I got popcorn and pizza and lots of soda, and there's a good movie on TV. Why don't you come over?" Cindy said.

"I can't. I gotta baby-sit my brothers and the baby," Amberlynn replied. "Plus, I gotta work on a science project."

"Oh, okay," Cindy said, abruptly hanging up the telephone and calling Jamee. Though Jamee had scolded her early in the day, Cindy was sure she would still come over if she could. Last year, when they were both in middle school, Jamee had a lot of problems.

19

First she got involved with an abusive guy from Bluford named Bobby Wallace, and then she ran away from home and nearly died in the process. During that whole time, Cindy had tried her best to support Jamee. Now Jamee always talked about someday returning the favor. Recently it seemed as if things with Jamee were better, while things in Cindy's life kept getting worse. Once Cindy joked about needing Jamee to help her out, and Jamee said, *"I got your back, Cindy. Remember that."*

"Hi, Jamee," Cindy said, glad Jamee answered the phone.

"Hey Cindy," Jamee said cheerfully, "what's up?"

"My mom is out tonight, and I was wondering if you want to come over and watch a movie with me. I got lots of popcorn and—"

"Girl, I'd come over if I could," Jamee said, "but my dad got a raise at work, and we're all goin' out to celebrate. Mom made reservations at this fancy restaurant. We're gettin' dressed up and everything. Maybe next time?"

"Yeah," Cindy responded sorely. She was jealous of Jamee. Sometimes Jamee complained about her family, but at least she had one. Sitting in her lonely apartment, Cindy would have traded places with Jamee in a heartbeat.

"Hey, are you coming to school tomorrow? I got so much to tell you."

"Yeah, I'm going," Cindy said, but in her heart she doubted it. "'Night, Jamee."

Cindy hung up, and an emptiness descended on her like a thick, bleak fog. "Nobody is coming over, Theo," Cindy said. The cat rolled over on the floor, yawned, and went to sleep.

Cindy debated if she should walk down to the sandwich shop at the corner. It was only 7:00, but after sunset, the neighborhood near her apartment could be dangerous, especially for someone walking alone.

Deciding to stay home, Cindy went to the fridge and found several TV dinners stacked in a corner of the half-empty freezer. She passed them up for an ice cream bar, returned to the recliner, and turned on the TV. A comedy was on about aliens who came to live on Earth.

Cindy felt like the aliens on the show, different from everyone around her. She had felt this way for years. When she was a young child, Cindy spent very little time with her mother. Years later, she learned Mom had been a drug addict. All Cindy remembered was that her mother would often stay locked in her bedroom for days. Whenever that happened, Aunt Shirley, Mom's older sister, would come over to take care of Cindy. She looked forward to Aunt Shirley's visits, even though it meant her mother would be unavailable for a while. Aunt Shirley made delicious apple-cinnamon cookies whenever she came over. *"The Lord will see us through this, Cindy. Yes he will,"* she would say as she baked. Often, Cindy would help with the cookies. Her favorite part was the batter, which Cindy liked to eat when Aunt Shirley was not looking.

Once, when Cindy was in elementary school, she stayed with Aunt Shirley for an entire summer, and Mom went into drug rehab. Cindy remembered that summer as her happiest. Each day she would go to the beach or the park with her aunt and play with the kids from the neighborhood. Then one day Mom took Cindy back, and for a while everything was great. Mom was drug-free and loving, and they were a real family. But when Cindy was twelve, Aunt Shirley got sick with breast cancer. Her health declined rapidly, and in a matter of months, she died.

Mom cried for days when Shirley died. Many months later, Mom sat Cindy down, confessed her former drug problems, and vowed she would never use drugs again. *"I'm going to get you a better life, baby,"* she had promised. Cindy remembered that conversation often as she sat in the lonely apartment. It was a special time in which she felt important to her mother—a feeling she no longer had.

Cindy noticed that their relationship began to change for the worse when her mother started dating. At first, Cindy thought her mother was happy to be going out. But after several breakups, she became increasingly frustrated. *"It ain't right for a woman my age not to have herself a man,"* she said one night, as she got ready to go out. At times, it seemed to Cindy that Mom was desperate. *"I ain't gettin' any younger, Cindy. I don't wanna be one of those women who end up livin' alone, like some old maid,"* she admitted after a particularly bad date.

Cindy tried to reassure her mother, but it seemed to her that Mom never listened. Instead, she would find another man. Once, she dated a guy named Eddie for a few months, but he turned out to be an alcoholic. Then she dated Steve, a married man who had five kids. Along the way, there were other men who were in the picture for such a short time that Cindy never got to know them. Then Raffie came along like a bad dream. Mom called him a "keeper" and said she was in love with him. She even admitted one night that she would like to marry him. The news sickened Cindy. She did not trust Raffie from the moment they met. A few times, she told her mother what she thought. But Mom always defended him.

"You never give Raffie a chance," she insisted. *"He's a sweetheart."* But as far as Cindy was concerned, there was nothing sweet about him. Ever since he arrived, Mom spent less time at home and paid less attention to Cindy. Even worse, Raffie could manipulate Mom into doing whatever he wanted. Sometimes Mom would cancel the rare plans she had with Cindy just to be with him. *He doesn't care one bit about anything but himself*, Cindy thought. She could not imagine anything worse than him being her stepfather.

Leaning back in the recliner, Cindy wondered where her mother and Raffie were. She figured they probably ended up at some noisy nightclub. Mom was probably laughing as if she did not have a care in the world. The more she envisioned her mother having a good time, the sadder Cindy became. Tears welled in her eyes. Turning the TV off, she went into her bedroom and flopped onto the bed. "Someday, Mom, you'll wish you didn't leave me alone all night," she murmured. "Someday you'll know you made a big mistake." The bitter thoughts gave Cindy a kind of comfort, and she drifted off to sleep.

In the morning, Cindy went to the bathroom and threw cold water on her face. She heard her mother in the kitchen making coffee. Cindy thought about her classes at Bluford—history, algebra, and English—and all the missed assignments she would have to make up. There was just no way she could catch up, so she decided to stay home from school again.

"Good morning, baby," Mom sang out cheerfully when Cindy arrived in the kitchen. "What kinda cereal do you want? I bought that variety pack you like, the one with all the little boxes."

Cindy chose a box of frosted corn flakes and dumped its contents into a bowl. Without a word, she poured milk onto the cereal. Grabbing her spoon, Cindy remembered how Aunt Shirley used to make homemade waffles with warm maple syrup. Everything tasted so much better when Aunt Shirley made it. She would sing gospel songs the entire time she was cooking.

"Raffie was so sweet last night. We had such a good time, Cindy," her mother beamed. "By the way, he's not mad at you anymore."

"Great," Cindy said smugly.

Just then, Cindy heard a knock on the door. She got up to answer it, grateful to escape another conversation about Raffie. Cindy found Jamee at the door adjusting her backpack. "Cindy! What're you doing in that old robe? It's time to get dressed for school," she cried.

"I'm not going to school today," Cindy said. "I know I said I would, but I changed my mind."

Then Cindy's mother stuck her head into the hallway and said, "Hi, Jamee."

"Mrs. Gibson, she has to go to school, doesn't she? Make her go!" Jamee pleaded.

Cindy's mother shrugged. "I keep tellin' her if she don't get an education, she's gonna end up just like me, waitin' tables for the rest of her life. But what am I supposed to do? I'm only a mother. Who listens to mothers anymore?" She sighed, as if she were commenting on a story she had heard on the evening news. "Good luck getting through to her, Jamee," she said, heading back to the kitchen.

"Cindy, get dressed and come to school," Jamee urged, tugging on Cindy's arm. "You can still make it to school before the first bell. You wanna be like those kids who hang out at the corners watching the lights change from green to red?"

"I have tons of work to make up. There's no way I can do it," Cindy wailed.

"Yes you can. The English project in Mr. Mitchell's class isn't due for a while. I'll be your partner. We can work together. I've done a lot of the work already. I'll help you in the other classes too . . . please, Cindy," Jamee begged. "Girl, you gotta go to school."

"Why can't you just leave me alone?" Cindy groaned. "Why you always tryin' to tell me what I should do? If my mom don't care, why should you?"

"Because we're tight. That's what friends do, right? When things were bad for me last year, you stuck with me, Cindy. When Bobby Wallace beat me up, you brought me here and helped me clean up so I could go home without my family knowin' what had happened."

"That's different," Cindy said, shrugging her shoulders.

"No, it's not. Now it's time for me to help you," Jamee replied. "Go change your clothes, and hurry up. We can still get there by the first bell."

Reluctantly, Cindy gave in. "Oh, okay. Anything to make you stop naggin' me. But, I'm telling you, don't count on me going tomorrow."

Cindy quickly washed, went into her bedroom and put on the jeans and the tank top that she had rediscovered the day before. Soon she and Jamee left the apartment building and headed towards Bluford.

As they reached the street, Cindy saw Harold Davis up ahead. She remembered the words his grandmother had said to her the day before. *"You have the prettiest hazel brown eyes."*

Walking to school silently with Jamee, Cindy worried about what her teachers would say about her many absences. She worried about her mother and what would become of her relationship with Raffie. But worse, she wondered if things between her and Mom would ever improve. Feeling a knot in her stomach, Cindy tried to push the worries from her mind. Again, Mrs. Davis's words echoed in her mind. *"Prettiest hazel-brown eyes."*

Cindy knew the words could not solve her problems, but she held them close to her heart as she walked through the tall steel doors of Bluford High School.

Chapter 3

When Cindy arrived at English class, Mr. Mitchell fixed his gaze on her. "Miss Gibson," he said, his voice seeming to catch on her last name. Cindy braced herself for criticism. "I need to see you after class."

Great, Cindy thought. *I'm back in school two minutes, and I'm already in trouble!* She knew he was going to lecture her for missing so much school. When Mr. Mitchell referred to a student as Mr. or Miss, it usually meant trouble.

During the entire class, Cindy worried. She kept looking at the clock, counting the minutes until Mr. Mitchell would yell at her. "Why did I let you drag me to school?" she whispered to Jamee towards the end of class. Jamee just shrugged.

When the bell finally rang, the room emptied quickly, leaving Cindy and Mr.

Mitchell. He was wearing a checkered green tie and a red shirt that contrasted with his dark skin.

"Uh," Cindy began, "I'm sorry I missed so much school, but see—"

"Excuse me, Cindy," said Mr. Mitchell, leaning back and pushing his glasses up on his nose, "but when you came to Bluford, you indicated cartooning as one of your interests. The other day, I was looking at last year's middle-school newspaper, and I found some of your work. It was great! You've got a lot of talent. So, I was thinking, the *Bluford Bugler* needs a cartoonist. What would you think of trying your hand at it?"

For an instant, Cindy turned numb. She had expected to be lectured, not offered a job. "Well . . . yeah, that'd be . . . I mean, sure, I'd love to do that," Cindy stammered. She had always loved to draw, but lately, with all the problems at home, she had sort of abandoned it.

"There's just one condition—you can never miss a deadline. If you promise a cartoon and don't deliver, you are off the paper. Are we clear on that?" Mr. Mitchell said crisply.

"Yeah, sure," Cindy said.

"Okay then. After school go see Ms.

Abbott. I already mentioned you to her. She's eager to have you on the staff. Good luck, Cindy."

"Thanks!" Cindy said, stunned. It was the first time since she came to Bluford that she felt excited by something. She couldn't wait to tell Jamee what had happened.

"Hopefully, I'll be seeing more of you in my class in the future," Mr. Mitchell added, as she walked towards the door.

Cindy nodded, knowing that he was referring to her poor attendance. "You will," she said with a smile. "Thanks, Mr. Mitchell."

At lunchtime, Jamee and Amberlynn squealed with excitement when Cindy shared the good news with them.

"That's great!" Jamee cheered. "One day, you'll be famous."

"You go, girl!" Amberlynn cheered.

"I just hope they like my drawings," Cindy said, feeling unsure of herself.

"Of course they will," Jamee replied, reaching for her soda, then taking a quick sip. "This is the best news ever."

"Yeah, I can't wait to see your first cartoon in the school paper," Amberlynn chimed in. "I'm gonna frame it."

Just then, Cindy noticed a boy across

the lunchroom watching her. At first, Cindy wasn't sure who he was—only that he was tall, with broad shoulders. But then she recognized his face.

"Is that who I think it is?" Cindy asked.

"Him?" Jamee said shaking her head. "That's Bobby Wallace, the one who tried to turn me into a punching bag."

"I can't stand the sight of him ever since I found out what he did to you," said Amberlynn, rolling her eyes disgustedly. "I see the way he sweet-talks girls in front of their lockers all the time, like he's so smooth."

"Well, he is smooth all right, I'll give him that," Jamee said. "But if they knew what I know, they'd stay far away from him."

"He looks different. I hardly recognize him," Cindy said, pretending not to notice him. Bobby continued to stare at her, and Cindy wasn't sure, but it looked as if he was smiling.

Amberlynn chuckled. "You been away from school so much, I'm surprised you remember what Bluford looks like. But all that's gonna change now that you're a big newspaper artist, right?"

"That's right, Amberlynn," Cindy said, laughing. "Soon you'll have to call my secretary if you want to see me." Cindy enjoyed the idea that at last she had something in her life that other people thought was cool. She wondered what her mother would say when she told her the news. She hoped Mom would be excited. Maybe, for once, she'd be proud. Maybe she would even skip a night with Raffie to spend time at home.

After school, Cindy went to Ms. Abbott's classroom. She was a pretty, dark-skinned woman who taught English and speech. She was also the advisor for the *Bluford Bugler*. Cindy liked her immediately because she seemed warm and enthusiastic.

"Remember, Cindy, you're on the newspaper staff now. Don't let me down," she said.

"No way, Ms. Abbott. I'm really excited about this," Cindy responded. "I wouldn't do anything to mess it up."

Ms. Abbott and Cindy discussed several ideas for upcoming issues of the paper. "Your first assignment," Ms. Abbott said, "is to draft a sketch to accompany an article on the cafeteria food." Cindy had ideas for the cartoon immediately, and she shared them with Ms. Abbott.

"They sound great! I can't wait to see what you come up with." Ms. Abbott smiled. "I can see why Mr. Mitchell recommended you."

Cindy was beaming when she left Ms. Abbott. School had been over for nearly a half hour, so most students had cleared out, except for those involved in after-school activities. As Cindy rounded the corner of a long corridor, she bumped into a student coming from the opposite direction. It was Pedro Ortiz, a six-foot-tall senior that everyone recognized. Even when she was in middle school, Cindy had heard many rumors that he was involved with gangs.

"Watch where you walkin', girl," he said as she bounced off his wide chest.

"Sorry," Cindy replied, turning away quickly. She did not know him at all, but something about him gave her the creeps. He seemed to lurk around Bluford, rarely speaking to anybody. She wondered what he was doing hanging around so late after school.

Cindy rushed outside to get away from Pedro. As she reached the Bluford parking lot, she heard a horn honking. She looked up to see a red Nissan not far away. Behind the wheel was Bobby Wallace. "Hey, baby, want a ride home?" he shouted.

Cindy looked around. Surely he wasn't talking to her! Guys didn't talk to her that way. No one other than Mom had ever called her "baby" before. She started to walk home, but then the horn sounded again. "Your name is Cindy, right?" Bobby asked.

"Yeah," Cindy said warily, remembering how Bobby had hit Jamee. Cindy did not trust any guy who could hit his girlfriend. "I think I'll walk home, thanks."

"You mean to tell me that you'd rather walk than ride?" Bobby said with a sly smile.

"I'd rather walk than ride with you," Cindy replied, picking up her pace.

"What's that supposed to mean?"

"Bobby Wallace, I ain't new at this school," Cindy retorted. "I know about what happened with you and Jamee Wills last year."

Bobby parked his car and jumped out. "Hey, Cindy, I know where you're comin' from, and I don't blame you for wantin' nothin' to do with me. Jamee

Wills has been dissin' me, but what she says ain't necessarily so, Cindy. We were both messed up last year. Me and Jamee both were doin' some crazy stuff. She's movin' on now, and so am I. Give a brotha a chance."

"Why should I?" Cindy asked, folding her arms across her chest. "Why should I give you a chance?"

"Because I want to get to know you better," Bobby replied, sounding sincere. "And I think you want to get to know me better, too. Just give me a chance."

Cindy hesitated. Bobby was very handsome, with dark eyes and broad shoulders. Cindy was flattered by his attention. "Come on," he urged.

Cindy was torn. She knew her friends would disapprove if she went with him, but they had all taken rides with boys before. No boy had ever talked to her like Bobby did. And he seemed so sincere. "I guess it'd be okay to ride home with you," Cindy said. "But you have to take me straight home."

"Deal," said Bobby. He smiled as they walked to his Nissan. And as they got into the car, he said with a wink, "You are looking good, girl."

Cindy blushed, embarrassed by his

attention. She was glad she was wearing the blue-ribbed tank top and close-fitting jeans. She smiled back at him, her heart pounding with excitement.

"I was real tight with Jamee last year, real tight," Bobby said. "She was old for her age. I mean, she didn't act like no middle schooler. She had a grudge against the world, and she was out to prove something. Well, we did drugs, both of us, and they messed with my mind real bad. Yeah, I got rough with her, but it was the drugs doin' the violence, Cindy. I swear it was the drugs, and now I'm clean. I ain't no fool. I wouldn't mess with no drugs again for no reason, and I wouldn't hit no girl. Never," Bobby said solemnly, pulling out of the school lot.

"She was really crazy about you, Bobby," Cindy said. "She cut out pictures of you playing football. She even made a scrapbook just to look at you when you weren't there."

"Well, I don't know about that, but I do know that she was crazy," Bobby said. "She was into shoplifting, and she ran away from home. Like I said, I give her credit for movin' on now. I give her a lot of credit for that."

Cindy enjoyed listening to Bobby. He seemed friendly and respectful, nothing like the violent person Jamee had described. She felt flattered to be with him, riding in his car.

Bobby pulled up in front of Scoops, an ice cream shop not far from Cindy's apartment. "Whatever you want, it's yours," Bobby said, reaching over and running his hand along Cindy's cheek. She was speechless. "I know you said straight home, but you ain't gonna stop a brotha from buyin' you some ice cream, are you?"

"Well . . . okay," Cindy said, smiling. His hand seemed strong but gentle. It was impossible to imagine him ever being violent. Cindy believed what he said. The drugs had made him a dangerous person, but he was different now.

"You just gotta try this mint cookie swirl," Bobby said. "I'll order us both one."

"Okay," Cindy said, going along with his suggestion.

Sitting in Bobby's car, Cindy felt touched by magic. She had not felt that way since she was five and played a fairy princess at a school play, wearing a sparkling tiara and silver slippers.

"This is really good," Cindy said, tasting the ice cream.

"What'd I tell you? I know all the cool spots. If you trust me, Cindy, we can have a real good time together."

As soon as they finished eating, Bobby dropped Cindy off at her apartment, and she went running up the stairs to bring her mother the good news. What a day it had been! Cindy could hardly believe all she would have missed if she had not gone to school. In one day, she had become a cartoonist for the school newspaper, and she had a handsome boy show interest in her. For once, she had something that might make her mother proud. She burst into the apartment eager to share the day's news.

"Mom," Cindy yelled as she pushed open the door. "I'm gonna be drawing cartoons for the school newspaper, and some guy . . . Mom?"

Her mother usually called to Cindy that she was in the kitchen or in the bedroom, but there was only silence now. It was 4:00. Mom was always home by 3:30 on Fridays.

"The laundry room," Cindy said to herself, snapping her fingers. She remembered that Mom always did laundry on Fridays after she got home from work. Cindy raced downstairs, yelling "Mom" as she approached the laundry room. But when she got there, the only person she saw was Harold, feeding change into one of the machines.

"Oh . . . hi," Cindy said, disappointed. "I was looking for my mom."

Harold looked shy and uncomfortable. In class when a teacher called on him, he often looked frightened. Cindy had never known someone who seemed more shy.

"I been down here for a half hour, and I haven't seen her," Harold said softly, not looking at Cindy when he talked.

"Are you sure?" Cindy asked.

"Yeah, I know your mom. She looks like you. She hasn't been down here since I got home from school," Harold said.

"Thanks," Cindy said bleakly. Heading back to the apartment, Cindy figured her mother must have gone to the store. She could not wait for her to return so she could tell her everything. Cindy decided to feed Theo and Cleo while she waited. As she entered the kitchen, she noticed a note taped to the refrigerator door. Cindy instantly recognized her mother's fancy handwriting. It read:

Cindy,

*Raffie won a free trip for two to
Vegas and he just sprung it on
me today. We had to leave right
away. I'll be home Sunday morning.
Plenty of TV dinners in the fridge.
Baby, I think my man is gonna
pop the question! Wish me luck!*

*Love and kisses,
Mom*

Cindy stared at the note, disbelief
and rage building within her.

"No!" she yelled aloud, yanking the
piece of paper off the refrigerator. *Mom
never did anything like this before,* she
thought, crumpling the note. *How could
she do this?* There had been some all-
nighters where her mother snuck back
in at dawn. But a whole weekend?
Never. Cindy quickly grabbed a can of
cat food and divided its contents
between the two bowls on the floor. Then
she sank into the recliner, her spirits
crumbling.

"I can't believe she did this, Theo,"
Cindy said. The cat started eating, and
Cindy's words were drowned by the
silence of the apartment. All the exciting

news she wanted to tell her mother instantly faded, leaving an aching emptiness in its place. She had to spend two more days alone in the dismal apartment. She would go to bed and wake up with nobody to even share cold cereal with, and the same would happen the next day. The silence in the apartment seemed to grow louder with each moment.

"Mo-ommm," Cindy moaned, "how come you don't care about me?" Hot tears welled in her eyes. "How come you don't love me?" Suddenly the doorbell rang. Cindy quickly wiped her eyes and walked to the front door, peering through the tiny glass peephole to see who was there. Rose Davis was standing in the hallway.

"It's me, honey," Rose said. Cindy opened the door and tried her best to smile.

"I hate to be bothering you, but that grandson of mine is giving me fits. You have that Mr. Mitchell for English class like he does, don't you?"

"Yes," Cindy answered leadenly, hoping Mrs. Davis would not know she had been crying.

"Well, Harold says that Mr. Mitchell is asking you to write one hundred pages for that report, and that don't make no sense to me. What high school student would need to write a hundred pages? Will you come explain the assignment to Harold?" Mrs. Davis asked.

"Okay," Cindy said. "I'll get my binder where I wrote down everything about the project."

Cindy got her binder and followed Mrs. Davis to her apartment. It looked a lot shabbier inside than her own place. The furniture was old and beat-up. But a delicious smell was coming from the kitchen.

"Gramma," Harold complained softly when he saw Cindy. "What'd you bother her for?"

"Well, child, ain't you been going on and on about the teacher wanting a hundred pages? Goodness sakes, I needed to get at the truth," Mrs. Davis said.

"Mr. Mitchell said our paper has to be ten pages but that we gotta read a book at least a hundred pages long," Cindy explained.

"Oh," Harold said. He did not look at Cindy. He stared at the paper in front of him as though he was trying to make a hole in it with his gaze.

"Cindy, honey, Harold told me you were looking for your momma. I saw her rushing outta here like the whole building was on fire. If she don't have time to make dinner, why don't you and her come and join us for dinner tonight? I'm cooking a whole mess of Cajun pork chops and mashed potatoes," Mrs. Davis said.

"My mom . . . she's gone . . . uh, I mean she's working late," Cindy replied, ashamed to admit her mother had run off to Vegas with her boyfriend. She especially did not want to tell that to Mrs. Davis, who sang in the church choir every Sunday.

"Well, then, it's settled," Mrs. Davis said with a big grin that plumped out her cheeks. "You're gonna eat with us tonight. Harold, go set an extra plate at the table."

"Thank you, Mrs. Davis," Cindy said. She was grateful for the invitation, not only because of the heavenly smells of pork chops, but mostly because she would not be eating a TV dinner by herself. "That's real nice of you," she added.

Mrs. Davis smiled. "Sit down and make yourself at home," she said. "If you want anything, ask Harold and he'll get it for you. I'm gonna finish dinner." Mrs. Davis turned and moved towards the stove.

Cindy walked over to the small kitchen table where Harold was setting a third place. He worked with his head down, as if his chin was stuck to the top of his chest.

Despite being in the Davises' warm apartment, Cindy couldn't stop thinking of her mother and the two lonely days ahead of her. She wondered if Mom even missed her. Probably not, she concluded.

Pushing back thoughts of her mother, she sat down and looked over at Harold. He was sitting across from her in complete silence.

Chapter 4

"Harold, who do you hang around with at school?" Cindy asked, trying to break the tension. Except in classes, she rarely saw Harold at Bluford.

"Hang around with?" Harold responded, staring at the table. "Nobody, I guess. I hang by myself mostly."

"How come?" Cindy asked.

Harold shrugged. "Guess I just haven't found the right people."

"I know what you mean," Cindy said. With the exception of Jamee and Amberlynn, Cindy did not hang out with anyone else. Again, the uncomfortable silence descended. Cindy tried to think of something to ask Harold, when he suddenly spoke up.

"Have you been sick?" he asked. "I haven't seen you in school as much, and I was wondering if you're okay."

"I'm fine," Cindy said, surprised that he noticed her absences. "I was sick for a few days, but I'm better now," Cindy lied. She did not want to tell Harold her problems, especially not with Mrs. Davis so close by.

Harold smiled. "I'm glad you're back," he said. "Feeling better, I mean."

Just then Mrs. Davis carried over a large plate of pork chops and an enormous bowl of mashed potatoes. "All right, I don't want anyone leavin' this table hungry," she said, filling Cindy's plate. It had been years since Cindy had eaten such wonderful homemade food.

As they ate, Cindy spoke about her new job drawing cartoons for the *Bluford Bugler*.

"Well, ain't that amazing! You draw pictures that make folks laugh! Child, that's a gift, a real gift," Mrs. Davis cried.

Harold was shoving mashed potatoes into his mouth as if he hadn't eaten in a week. "Uhmmm-mmm," he said.

"It's just a high school paper," Cindy explained, "but it's kinda fun. It's the only thing I've ever done that's, you know, special. In middle school this one teacher saw me sketching a cartoon, and when he saw it he laughed, he really laughed."

48

"You have got to show me your drawings, Cindy. I love to laugh," Mrs. Davis said. "First thing I do when the paper comes is look at the cartoons. The front of the paper is so full of bad news . . . people gettin' shot, crime and drugs all over the place. Lord, we need some laughter in our lives."

"I put my cartoons from middle school in a scrapbook, Mrs. Davis. I'll show it to you one day," Cindy promised.

After dinner, Mrs. Davis embraced Cindy warmly. "I'm so glad you came over tonight," Mrs. Davis said. Being hugged by the old woman was like being wrapped in a favorite warm blanket. It seemed like years since her mother had given her such a hug.

As Cindy walked back to her dark apartment, her frustration with Mom returned. *A mother ought to love her child more than her boyfriend,* Cindy thought, *especially if her boyfriend is a dog like Raffie Whitaker.*

Cindy wondered what she would do if Mom came home with an engagement ring. She liked the idea of running away. She could just jump on a bus and get as far from Raffie as possible. Then maybe her mother would feel guilty and miss her. But what if Mom let her run away and never bothered to find her? That was the scariest thought of all.

Sitting in the quiet living room, Cindy noticed how different her apartment was from Harold's. Where the Davis living room was warmly lit and comfortable, hers seemed stark and barren. And Mrs. Davis's kitchen—neatly crowded with hanging pots and filled with the aroma of countless homemade meals—was nothing like Cindy's, a spartan room used mainly to heat TV dinners.

Recently, Mom had mentioned the need to decorate the apartment, but Cindy just rolled her eyes at the suggestion. She suspected the reason Mom even cared was because of Raffie. A few months ago he bought a gift for the apartment, a hideous clown sculpture that now stood on the coffee table in front of her.

"Raffie said this gives the room character," Mom said proudly as she positioned the sculpture on the table. Cindy thought it looked like something picked up for two dollars at a yard sale, but Mom treated it like a priceless object.

Cindy stared at the clown. Right about now, she figured Mom and Raffie were in Las Vegas strolling down some flashy street, seeing a hotel made to look like New York or Egypt or something. Cindy pictured Raffie, swaggering along with his ugly gold chains, his gold bracelets, and his awful leather pants. The thought that Raffie might possibly become her stepfather knotted Cindy's stomach.

She leaned towards the coffee table and picked up the clown. Its face was contorted into an ugly smirk that reminded her of Raffie. Cindy imagined how good it would feel to hold it over her head and smash it down on the floor, shattering it into a thousand pieces. Her eyes moved to the small card taped to the base of the clown—

To my number one lady, Lori,
from Ramblin' Raffie.

Cindy's hands trembled as she set the clown back down. Someday when she knew for sure that her mother did not love her, she would smash it. All that kept her from hurling the clown onto the floor was the fading hope that Mom still cared about her.

Would she be happier without me? Cindy asked herself. Then Mom would be free to spend all her time with Raffie. *Is that what she really wants?* Cindy did not know what she would do if her fears were true, if her mother did not love her.

She stared at the clown again. It appeared to grin back at her with a wicked, mocking smile.

"Please, Mom, come home," she said softly over and over, finally falling asleep on the lumpy old couch.

Amberlynn called early Saturday morning. "Cindy, you won't believe the lie Natalie Wallace is telling people. She said you went out on a date with her brother, Bobby."

"We just went out for ice cream, that's all," Cindy said. "It wasn't a date."

"So, you *were* in his car?" Amberlynn demanded.

"Yeah. So what?" Cindy shot back. "You make it sound like it's a big deal."

"It *is* a big deal, Cindy. You know what he did to Jamee," Amberlynn cried. "I just can't believe you'd even give him the time of day after all that happened last year. Think of how upset Jamee's gonna be when she hears about this."

"What's she gonna be upset about?" Cindy replied. "She dumped Bobby a long time ago."

"Have you forgotten why?" Amberlynn asked, her voice rising to a high pitch. "You were there, Cindy! You remember what he did to her! I can't believe you would even—"

"Amberlynn, all that stuff's in the past," Cindy responded with a dramatic sigh. "Just let it go."

Let it go?!" Amberlynn exclaimed. "Bobby Wallace beat up one of our best friends and almost ruined her life. How am I supposed to let that go? And how can you ride around with him like nothing ever happened?"

"He's changed," Cindy said. "Bobby admitted he did bad things, but he's different now. Like your brother, Roylin. He's changed, hasn't he?"

"Cindy, that's different. Roylin may have gotten into trouble a few times, but he never hung out with drug dealers, and he never beat on no girls either," Amberlynn said.

"Well, I think you need to mind your own business," Cindy snapped. "That's what I think."

"Girl, you don't have to talk like that to me," Amberlynn responded. "I'm just lookin' out for you, okay?"

"Well, I can look out for myself. Anyway, I gotta go now," Cindy said. "Mom's here." Cindy was lying, but she did not want to listen to more lecturing about Bobby Wallace. Bobby was the one reason Cindy was not totally depressed about being left alone for the entire weekend. She was not about to let Amberlynn take that away.

Cindy still could not believe how nice Bobby had been to her yesterday. *Could he actually like me?* she wondered. She decided to head over to Bluford to watch the Buccaneers at football practice. She knew Bobby would be there.

Cindy ran to her bedroom and looked for something nice to wear. She chose a pair of snug jeans and a clingy navy blue v-neck T-shirt. *Bobby will like me in this,* she thought. She quickly got dressed and headed over to Bluford, hoping to catch Bobby's eye.

When Cindy reached the football field, the team was in a huddle. She searched to find Bobby but did not see him right away. Then, when she saw the name WALLACE on the back of a jersey, her heart started pounding.

Cindy stepped onto the bleachers, hoping to get a spot where Bobby would notice her. A small crowd of spectators was gathered on the bleachers. Cindy spotted Natalie Wallace waving in her direction.

"Hi," Natalie called out. "How you doin', Cindy?"

"Okay," Cindy called back. Natalie had never talked to her before. But maybe now that Cindy and Bobby were friends, things would be different. Cindy walked over to where Natalie was sitting and joined her. She always thought Natalie was one of the prettiest girls at Bluford.

"I like to watch my brother show off," Natalie said with a smile. Cindy could not believe that Natalie was talking to her, let alone allowing her to sit beside her on the bleachers. "You here to do the same thing?" she asked with a playful grin.

"Maybe," Cindy replied, unsure what else to say.

"Yep, my brother sure moves fast," Natalie said, getting up from her seat. Practice was over, and Cindy was left wondering whether she was referring to her brother on the football field or in some other way.

Cindy watched as the team left the field. She hoped Bobby had seen her in the bleachers. She just had to see him. Unsure what else to do, she decided to wait for him in the parking lot. After a few minutes, Bobby came out of the school and headed towards his car.

"You looked great, Bobby," Cindy said as he approached. "No wonder everybody says you're gonna be a big football star."

"Hey, you came to watch me practice?" Bobby replied with a look of pleasant surprise. "You're okay, girl. Come on, let's go grab something to eat."

Beaming, Cindy hurried towards the passenger door. She couldn't wait to talk to him. "They're having a special at Niko's Pizza Place, two slices for the price of—"

"I don't like that place," Bobby interjected. "Too many lame fools hang out there. There's a Chinese takeout place I like. Let's go there."

When Cindy got in the car, she turned to Bobby and said, "Guess what happened yesterday? Ms. Abbott chose me as an artist for the *Bluford Bugler.* I just found out—"

"Really?" Bobby said. "You go to most of the football games, Cindy?"

"Sometimes," Cindy answered.

"Well now that we're tight, you gotta come to all the games," Bobby insisted. "From now on, I'm gonna look for you whenever I'm on the field. Never mind those cheerleaders. Last time I seen so many dogs was at the pound!" Bobby joked.

"So Mr. Mitchell told me about the newspaper opening on Friday and—"

"Hey, Cindy, were you at last year's game against Lincoln? That was one of my best games."

"No. I haven't been to that many games."

"Well, you gotta come to every one from now on, Cindy. That's an order," Bobby said with a smile.

Cindy smiled back, slightly disappointed that Bobby did not give her a chance to share her good news with him. Bobby pulled his Nissan into the parking lot of the Chinese takeout. "Do they have sweet and sour chicken?" Cindy asked. "That's my favorite. I always get that."

"Yeah, but the orange chicken is what you want, that's the best," Bobby said as they entered the restaurant. Then he ordered two orange chicken dishes for them. He looked at Cindy and smiled. She smiled back at him weakly. Bobby certainly wanted things his way, she thought. But it was only food, and it felt nice to have him order for her.

"That sounds good," Cindy responded. "I can't wait to try it."

"Stick with me, girl," Bobby said. "I know where everything's happenin'. I got friends at all the cool places, and I know how to have fun. Trust me," Bobby said. "Hey, what time you gotta be home, Cinderella?"

Cindy smiled. Nobody had ever called her "Cinderella" before. It made her feel special, even beautiful. For once, her name did not sound so ugly. Cindy was so delighted by the nickname that she decided to tell Bobby the truth. "Mom's gonna be gone all day. I don't have to be home early," she said.

"For real?" Bobby said with a glimmer in his eyes. "Then let's have some fun."

After lunch, Bobby drove to an old rowhome in a rundown part of town where some of his older friends lived. "Don't let the looks of the place throw you. Nothing bad happens here," Bobby explained. "This is where we come to chill out—you know, listen to some music, dance, smoke a little weed."

Cindy grew a little nervous. She had smoked marijuana once in middle school with Jamee and some others. Though a few kids seemed to enjoy it, marijuana only made Cindy feel hazy and numb. Weed was a small deal compared to other drugs. Last year one of her classmates overdosed on heroin and almost died. Ever since, Cindy stayed far away from all drugs.

As she walked up the stairs to the house, Cindy felt her heart start to pound. She worried that kids would be doing drugs and would pressure her to do them too. If Bobby smoked weed, would she have to do it too? If she said "no" the way teachers always instructed, would he take her back home and never speak to her again?

Bobby led her into a tiny room where sheets hung in front of the windows as makeshift curtains. Against the far wall was a rumpled, stained sofa the color of a green beer bottle. "Have a seat, beautiful," he said, gesturing towards the sofa. "I'll be right back." He smiled before disappearing into another room. Cindy was comforted by his friendly words.

Bobby returned carrying a bottle of wine in one hand and two plastic cups in the other. "You drink wine, don't you?" he asked with a wide smile.

"Sure," Cindy said. It was true she had tasted wine a few times at family meals, but she never liked it. Bobby opened the bottle and filled Cindy's cup.

Cindy sipped the red wine slowly. She did not like its sharp acid taste, but she pretended to enjoy it. She knew drinking was dangerous, especially around people you don't know too well. But she wanted Bobby to think she was cool. Reluctantly, she took another tiny sip of the wine.

"You scared your mom'll get on your case if she finds out you were drinkin'?" Bobby asked.

"No, she don't care what I do," Cindy replied bluntly. "She ain't never around much anyway, so I basically do whatever I want." As she spoke, Cindy wondered where her mother was at the moment and whether she would get mad if she found out Cindy was in a strange house drinking wine with a boy. Cindy liked the fact that she was doing something that would upset Mom. In some small way, she was getting back at her for going to Vegas. Cindy grabbed the cup and took another sip.

"Yeah, I know what you mean," Bobby said. "My old man, he's got lung trouble. He sits around all day sucking up oxygen. One of those tanks, you know? That and yelling for Mom to wait on him. Mom's so busy doing for him and working downtown, cleaning bathrooms, she got no time to ride hard on me and Nat. That's what Mom does. Cleans johns." Bobby laughed bitterly, staring at the wine bottle as he spoke. "Know what, babe? I'm gonna get me some real money one of these days. Not chump change like they pay down at the car wash. Then Mom won't be cleanin' no toilets."

Cindy respected what Bobby said. Although she felt uncomfortable being in the house, she liked being with him. He made her feel important because he trusted her so much. The more he spoke, the closer she felt to him.

"My old man," Bobby continued, "he was a mean old cuss in his younger days. I remember him coming in the house and wanting food on the table, like right now. When Mom didn't hop to it, she got it right in the mouth. She don't hold it against him, though." Bobby shook his head. "Ain't that something?

She still takin' care of him today, no matter how mean he treats her. Girls today aren't like that. You get a little mean 'cause you're having a bad day, and they just walk out on you. Girls today don't know nothin' about loyalty." Bobby smiled at Cindy and rubbed her cheek gently with the back of his hand. "But you ain't that kind of girl. I can tell."

Just then, Cindy heard the footsteps and voices of other people. She grabbed hold of Bobby's arm. "Did you hear that?" she asked fearfully. "There's somebody else here."

"Calm down, girl. Let's go see who it is," Bobby said, rising to his feet.

"But, it could be trouble. Maybe we should leave," Cindy said nervously.

"Ain't no trouble I can't handle," Bobby replied.

The voices were coming from the basement. Cindy didn't want to go down there, but Bobby did. She was not about to be left alone in that strange place, so she followed him.

"Relax, you're in good hands," he assured her.

Cindy wanted to believe him, but she just didn't feel safe in the old house. She wished she and Bobby were someplace else, like walking along a beautiful beach. She imagined him with his arm around her, and how nice it would be to get away from the city. But her visions were shattered by the reality in front of her—that she and Bobby were heading towards a group of strangers in an unfamiliar basement.

Chapter 5

The large basement of the house was already clouded with cigarette and marijuana smoke. On a far wall, the words "No Exit" were spray-painted in red, black and silver letters the size of house windows. Breathing in the pungent smoke, Cindy started to cough. Holding her hand, Bobby led her into the room.

"It's all right," he whispered. "I won't let nothin' happen to you."

Cindy squinted and noticed two blurry figures sitting close together. As she and Bobby moved further into the room, someone turned on thumping rap music that made conversation almost impossible. As Cindy watched, the two guys in the corner began heating heroin with a lit match. She had heard about people doing that, but she had never seen it. One of the boys rolled up his sleeve, and the other guy wrapped a belt around the first guy's arm. Cindy watched in horror as the one guy plunged a needle into the other's forearm, and his veins jumped out like fat wet noodles.

"What's up, Bobby?" said the guy holding the needle.

Cindy was bothered that Bobby knew such a person. She wondered how close they were. Although Bobby didn't answer the guy, he did nod at him in recognition.

"That's Omar, and the guy next to him is T-Bone," Bobby whispered.

"Bobby, let's get out of here," Cindy pleaded.

Omar shot himself up and was soon spaced out as well. The drugs seemed to sweep over the young men in waves. For a second, they seemed normal, and then abruptly their eyes snapped shut, their knees trembled, and drool snaked down their chins. Cindy felt like she might throw up.

"I hate this place, Bobby. I want to go, now!" Cindy demanded. She did not care what Bobby thought of her. She just wanted to get out of the house.

Bobby took her hand and led her out the front door. Taking a deep breath of fresh air, Cindy was grateful to be out-side again, but she was shaken by what she had just seen. She glanced over at Bobby. He was watching her.

"How do you know those guys?" she asked.

"Oh, they both used to go to Bluford," he said. "Omar and T-Bone used to play football back in the day. Then they got hooked on drugs."

"That's too bad," she replied, still unsettled by her experience.

"Some people get strung out," Bobby added, "but not me. They're junkies, but I ain't about that. I used to get high on weekends, but it was never on the heavy stuff."

"I'm glad," Cindy said. She appreciat-ed his honesty. But in her mind, she kept seeing the look on the boys' faces as the drugs rushed into their bodies.

"You ever shoot up, Cindy?" he asked, snapping her out of her thoughts.

"No!" Cindy exclaimed. She was embarrassed at how loud her response was, but she could not hide how uncom-fortable she felt. She was certain Bobby thought she was naive and stupid, the kind of girl that guys like him were never interested in. "Look, Bobby, I'm sorry. But can we just get outta here?" she pleaded.

"Sure," he said, putting his arm around her.

As they silently made their way to his car, Cindy was grateful that Bobby did not tease or criticize her for the way she acted. Even if he did know the guys in the basement, he was nothing like them.

"You're a lot nicer than some kids been saying, Bobby," Cindy said.

"What've I been trying to tell you? I ain't a bad guy, Cindy," Bobby declared as he started the car.

After pulling in front of Cindy's apartment, Bobby caressed her cheek and said, "Maybe I'm goin' a little too fast, huh? I do that sometimes when I really like somebody. I don't want to push you. I know we ain't been tight all that long, but I want you to have something." Bobby pulled a jacket from the back seat and put it around Cindy's shoulders.

"Your varsity jacket!" Cindy gasped. She could not believe what was happening. *This makes it official,* Cindy thought. If she wore the jacket to Bluford, everyone in the school would know she really was Bobby Wallace's girl. "Are you serious?" she asked, unable to contain her excitement.

"I want you to wear it, Cindy," Bobby said. "Because you're special to me."

"Oh Bobby, thank you!" Cindy screamed and kissed him on the lips. When she got out of his car, she turned and looked at him, unable to stop herself from smiling.

"I'll see you in school on Monday," he said. Cindy waved as he drove off.

When Cindy reached her apartment door, Rose Davis stepped out into the hallway. "Praise the Lord! You all right, child?" she asked.

"Sure, I'm fine," Cindy said. "Why?"

"Child, you been gone all day. I knocked on your door and there was nobody home. Where's your momma?"

Cindy had not expected Mrs. Davis to be so concerned about her. "Mom's on a . . . a business trip," Cindy lied.

"Honeychild, I'm an old woman, and a lot of this modern life is way over my head. But I got sense enough to know that a mother ought not leave her fifteen-year-old daughter all by herself for all this time."

Cindy shrugged. Ordinarily she

would have defended her mother from anyone's criticism. But there was something about Mrs. Davis that showed she really cared, and it felt good to have someone worry about her. "Mom is off with her boyfriend," Cindy admitted. "Something came up suddenly, and she just went."

"Hmmph," Mrs. Davis grunted, shaking her head side to side in disbelief. "Child, would you like some hot chocolate and fresh-baked raisin cookies?"

"That sounds real good," Cindy said, happy to talk to somebody and grateful not to have to return to her lonely apartment.

As Cindy sat at the kitchen table, Mrs. Davis asked, "When your momma getting back?"

"Tomorrow morning," Cindy said.

"Tomorrow! She left you all weekend?"

"It's okay," Cindy said, nibbling on a cookie still soft and warm from the oven.

"You been out with your boyfriend all day, haven't you?" Mrs. Davis asked.

"Yeah," Cindy said, smiling. "He gave me his Bluford varsity jacket. Look, isn't it cool? When boys let you wear their jackets, it means they really like you."

"Well some things haven't changed," Mrs. Davis said, smiling. "When I was a girl, if a boy went off to the army, he'd leave you with things to remember him by. The man I ended up marryin' gave me something special the day he left for the army. It was a ring that belonged to his father, and I cherished it every day."

"Bobby hasn't given me a ring yet," Cindy replied. "But maybe he will."

"Honey, don't be rushin' nothing," Mrs. Davis gently warned.

Cindy smiled, feeling silly for a moment.

"Child, have you got a grandma?"

"I used to, but she passed away when I was little," Cindy answered. "I hardly remember her."

"Well, let me be your grandma then. You can call me Grandma Rose, or just Grandma," Mrs. Davis said.

"Thanks, Mrs. Davis," Cindy said, grateful to the kind old woman. "I mean, Grandma Rose."

Mrs. Davis smiled warmly as she served the hot chocolate. "Now, tell me all about your boyfriend," she said, sitting down across from Cindy.

"He's really nice," Cindy began. "His name is Bobby Wallace and—"

"Harold has told me about that Bobby Wallace," Mrs. Davis interjected, frowning. "He has a very bad reputation, honey."

"People just don't understand him, Grandma Rose. Bobby has changed. He doesn't do bad stuff anymore. You believe people can change, don't you? It's like they always say in church. People can repent and change, and we are supposed to forgive them, right?"

"Yes, Cindy, I do believe in that, but folks have to really and truly change in their hearts. Sometimes they put on nice behavior, but deep down they haven't changed at all," Mrs. Davis said. "So you gotta be real careful, child, 'cause you're precious."

You're precious. The words echoed in Cindy's mind. She had been starved for kind words for so long that they were like a burst of rain on parched soil, spilling over instead of sinking in.

"I ain't precious," she said, thinking of her mother and Raffie. "I know that—"

"Hush your mouth," Mrs. Davis said sternly. "You are a beautiful child of the Lord, and you deserve a young man as fine as you. Don't let me ever hear you disrespecting yourself, child, you under-

71

stand? I won't stand for it." As she spoke, Mrs. Davis put her thick arms around Cindy and gave her a warm hug. Nestled amidst the scent of fresh cookies and dish soap, Cindy felt loved and protected.

"Thank you," Cindy said softly as Mrs. Davis gradually relaxed her strong embrace.

"I'm here for you, child," Mrs. Davis said. "Don't you forget that."

"Thank you, Grandma Rose," Cindy said before walking back to her apartment.

Alone in her room, Cindy busied herself with ideas for cartoons for the *Bluford Bugler.* She had to get her mind off the prospect of another night by herself in the gloomy apartment. Her mother would not be home until the next morning. Then she would go right to bed and sleep until the afternoon when she had to go to work.

Cindy wondered if her mother would be wearing a ring on her finger, a ring from Raffie with his jangling gold chains.

Cindy stayed up until midnight sketching cartoon ideas. Then she got dressed for bed, placed Bobby's jacket on a nearby chair, and crawled under her covers. Before falling asleep, she grabbed Bobby's jacket and held it next to her. It smelled like the musky cologne Bobby wore. She fell asleep holding one sleeve next to her cheek.

Cindy woke up to the smell of brewing coffee.

"Mom?" Cindy cried, jumping from bed and stumbling into the hallway in her bare feet.

"I'm in the kitchen," her mother called.

As she entered the kitchen half asleep, Cindy remembered how angry she was at her mother. "Well, you finally got back, huh?" she said sitting at the small table. Despite how happy and relieved she was that her mother was home, Cindy was unable to smile or say anything nice to her.

"Well, that's a nice welcome. What's your problem?" her mother snapped.

"It was really mean of you to leave like that for two days," Cindy said bitterly. "I couldn't believe you'd do that."

"Oh Cindy, give me a break! You're fifteen years old! You're always complaining that I don't give you enough credit for being grown-up. Well, now I did. I trusted you to behave yourself with nobody breathing down your neck, and that's a compliment that you ought to appreciate. Aren't you always saying 'Mo-om, I'm fifteen years old,'" her mother said with a whiny, childish voice. "'Mo-om, I'm not a baby anymore.'"

Cindy's rage grew. Mom was not even apologetic. She acted as if she had done nothing wrong. "I spent the whole time with my boyfriend," she said spitefully.

"Girl, don't lie to me. I know you don't have a boyfriend," her mother said, pouring a cup of coffee.

"I do now," Cindy cried. "And we were together all weekend, drinking and kissing and stuff. Then he gave me his varsity jacket. I guess he loves me, or he wouldn't have given it to me."

Cindy's mother turned sharply, spilling coffee on the table. "You better watch your mouth!" she yelled. "Do you want a good slap across your face? You keep talking like that, and that's just what you'll get, girl."

Cindy sat down at the table and sulked. She didn't see a ring on her mother's finger, and that consoled her. *Raffie probably found another excuse to push it off again,* Cindy thought. They had been dating now for a year, and Mom hoped to get married, but Raffie always had a reason why it had to be postponed.

"So," Cindy said at last, "did you and the creep have a good time?"

"You say another bad thing to me this morning, and I'll slap you silly. You hear me?" Mom growled. "I am tired of you dissing Raffie. He's a fine man. Whatever happens with me and him is none of your business."

"He didn't give you a ring, did he?" Cindy asked.

"I told you it was none of your business."

"He won't give you one either," Cindy persisted. "And you should be glad too. Who wants Raffie for a husband? I sure don't want him for a stepfather. I'd run away if you ever married him, that's what I'd—"

Mom's hand struck Cindy on the side of her cheek. The slap was not hard, but it stung Cindy's face. It was the first time in years Mom had hit her. She looked at her mother in disbelief.

"I told you I didn't wanna hear no more from you!" Mom said. "I'm gonna lie down and get some sleep now, and I don't want to hear your voice. Go do your homework or whatever. You make me

75

wish I didn't come home." Mom stomped down the hall to her bedroom and slammed the door.

Cindy remained at the kitchen table. She put her hand over the spot her mother had hit, rested her head down on the tabletop and cried. She did not want to fight with Mom. She had missed her so much. What Cindy wanted more than anything was to tell Mom about her new job on the school paper, her talk with Mr. Mitchell, and, of course, Bobby Wallace. But instead, she had spoiled what little time they had together by fighting.

Cindy said nothing as the tears rolled down her cheeks. She kept thinking her mother would hear her crying and come rushing out and put her arms around her and say, "Baby, I'm sorry. I'm sorry I went off with Raffie, and I am sorry for slapping you. Forgive me?"

But she didn't. Tears never changed anything, Cindy thought. Her eyes ached, her head throbbed, and her nose burned. But in the end nothing was changed. Nothing was any different.

Around 10:00, the phone rang and Cindy rushed to answer it, hoping it was Bobby.

"Hi Cindy, it's me," Jamee said, "My

sister has the car and we're going to the mall. Wanna come?"

"Yeah," Cindy said, eager to get out of the apartment. She pulled on clean jeans and a tank top and ran downstairs to wait for the car. She hoped Jamee would not criticize her for dating Bobby Wallace. Cindy was certain Jamee knew by now. Amberlynn probably told her everything.

Darcy and Jamee pulled up in an old beige Ford. "Isn't it great?" Darcy said, sitting at the wheel. She was a junior with a new driver's license, and she shared the car with her mother. Cindy could not wait for the day when she had a car of her own. She would drive far away and maybe never even come back.

"I wish I could drive," Cindy said. "My mom probably wouldn't let me borrow her car, though," she said, climbing into the car.

"You're only fifteen," Darcy added. "Besides, I'm seventeen, and the only time I get to drive is when my mother isn't working. Believe me, I know how it feels to be trapped at home," Darcy said, pulling out into the street.

"Cindy, are you really going out with Bobby Wallace?" Jamee asked suddenly.

Cindy took a deep breath. "Listen, Jamee. I know what you're thinking, but it's not like that. Bobby isn't the same person he was when you went out with him."

"But how do you know that for sure?" Jamee asked indignantly. "And besides, Cindy, don't you think it's a little rude of you to go after some guy that I used to date?"

"Rude?" Cindy repeated. "I don't see anything rude about it. I mean, you two were together so long ago."

"Like just last year," Jamee said quickly. "That's beside the point, Cindy. You know what I went through with Bobby. You know what he did to me. And still you're going out with him."

"Jamee, I don't need nobody tryin' to mind my business for me. Now I already told Amberlynn to—"

"Both of you relax," Darcy cut in, turning away from the steering wheel to glance at Cindy. "Jamee's just worried about you, that's all. And so am I. Don't forget that Bobby beat Jamee up, and he threatened me. Any boy who treats girls like that is dangerous. I don't know what makes you think he's changed so much," Darcy explained.

"Yeah," Jamee spoke up, "that's what I'm trying to say. I don't want you going through what happened to me. This isn't about you dating my ex, Cindy. It's about you being safe."

"Jamee, I appreciate what you're saying," Cindy said, cooling down. "You too, Darcy. But you just don't know Bobby like I do. He's a good guy now."

"That boy was crazy last year," Jamee said somberly.

"Yeah, but so were you," Darcy interjected. Jamee flashed Darcy a quick glare.

"Seriously, Cindy," Jamee said, "What makes you think he's any different now?"

"He said he was doing drugs last year and that messed up his mind. Now he's clean, and he's really nice," Cindy said.

"Just be careful," Darcy warned. "Take things real slow, Cindy."

"Doesn't your mom mind you hanging out with Bobby, knowing his rep?" Jamee asked.

"My mom doesn't have a clue about anything I do. She lets me do whatever I want," Cindy said.

"I wish my mom was like that," Jamee said.

"Don't be stupid, Jamee," Darcy grumbled. "Anyway, Cindy, your mom wouldn't want you dating Bobby if she knew what kind of guy he was."

"Yeah, well she's got no room to talk right now," Cindy replied, leaning back in the seat as they drove into the parking lot of the mall. She was not in the mood to talk about her mother. Instead, she wanted to buy some new things. She had forty dollars her mother had given her weeks ago for school clothes. She had not spent it at the time because she didn't care much for school or what she wore. But now she had a reason to shop. She wanted to be pretty for Bobby. She wanted to put a big smile on his face.

As the girls walked towards the mall, Darcy kept talking about how her mother, an ER nurse, was determined to make Darcy's prom dress. "I told her she doesn't have time, but she won't listen," Darcy said. "She says Grandma made her first party dress, and she wants to do the same for me." A pang of jealousy struck Cindy. She wished she had a close family like Darcy and Jamee's.

"Know what?" Cindy said, bitterness sweeping over her. "My mom left town Friday night, and she didn't get back till this morning. No joke. I was alone all that time 'cause she was with her boyfriend Raffie. All he ever does is insult me," Cindy added, fighting back tears of anger and hurt. "He lies to my mom about it, and she believes him over me. He drives his new Mercedes and wears gold chains and earrings. I think he looks like a big fool, but he thinks he's the man. Mom is crazy about him. It's like if Raffie and I were drowning, she'd go save him and let me drown."

"Cindy," Jamee said, "that's stupid. Your mom doesn't think that."

"Don't you try to tell me how my mother is! You don't live with me, so how would you know? Not everyone's family is as perfect as yours," Cindy yelled, angered at how Jamee denied what she lived through each day. "I'm telling you, she doesn't care about me. She wasn't always this way. I guess being in love with somebody is like being on drugs or something. Ever since Raffie came along, she's been different. It's like she wishes I would just go away so she wouldn't have to deal with me no more." Cindy looked down at her fingernails. Jamee and Darcy remained silent.

"Know what else?" Cindy said, her voice trembling. "I don't care either. I don't care if Mom doesn't love me, not anymore. I don't need her. I just need Bobby. I think he loves me, you guys. He calls me Cinderella, and he really loves me."

Jamee threw an arm around Cindy. "I'm sorry, girl," she said. "I'm not gonna tell you I'm happy about you and Bobby. But no matter what, I will always be here for you. So will Amberlynn—"

"And me too," Darcy cut in.

"We'll love you, with or without Bobby Wallace," Jamee said, pulling Cindy close to her and giving her a warm hug.

Darcy placed her hand on Cindy's back then. "Come on, Cindy. Let's shop till we drop!"

Together they walked into the mall without a word, the three girls with their arms around each other.

Chapter 6

The girls headed straight to their favorite clothing store, Fashion Central.

"Did you see what Latasha was wearing on Friday?" Jamee asked. "Didn't she look good?"

"Latasha?" Darcy scoffed. "If you ask me, that shirt was just too small. How is she ever gonna be taken seriously with her belly all exposed like that?"

"I thought she looked nice," Cindy replied. "Anyway, guys seemed to like what she was wearing."

Darcy laughed. "You two need to get over that," she said. "What guys want is not always best for you. Besides, when you get to be juniors, you'll be so busy working and looking for college money that you won't even care about clothes."

Cindy noticed Jamee rolling her eyes at her sister's comment. "Hey, do you like these shoes?" Jamee asked, holding up a pair of leather sneakers. "I saw a girl wearing them in a new music video."

"Oh, I love them!" Cindy cried. "But they cost eighty dollars. There's no way I can afford that."

"Look," Darcy shouted, "the stuff on this rack is sixty percent off."

The two girls rushed over, and Cindy grabbed an off-white sleeveless top. "It's my size, and it's only seven dollars! I can get two of these and a pair of pants," Cindy exclaimed, grabbing a number of inexpensive items off the shelves.

"Jamee," Darcy said as she searched through the rack, "did you tell Cindy about our Halloween party?"

"No, not yet," Jamee replied, examining a gray ribbed top.

"What party?" Cindy asked.

"Were having some friends over for Halloween," Darcy explained. "I told Jamee to invite you and Amberlynn. We're gonna watch scary movies and eat tons of junk food. It'll be great."

"Yeah Cindy, you gotta come over," Jamee added.

"We'll see," Cindy replied. "I don't know what Bobby's planning that night. He might want to do something."

Jamee rolled her eyes but said nothing. Cindy pretended not to notice her reaction.

"Well," Darcy said with a pleasant smile. "Just know you're invited. It's up to you whether or not you come over."

"Thanks," Cindy mumbled, trying not to be bothered by Jamee's silence.

For the rest of the afternoon, the girls wandered around the mall looking at clothes, listening to music, and eating at the food court. Cindy bought three tops and a pair of pants with her money, and by the time she got home, her mother had already left for work. It was just as well, Cindy thought. All they would have done is bicker some more. Cindy went right to her room to try on her new clothes.

Looking in the mirror, Cindy liked what she saw. Her new purple shirt and black pants fit her body perfectly. She could hardly wait to see Bobby's reaction when he saw her in them. She went through her entire closet trying on outfits she thought Bobby would like.

Cindy had never thought much of her body. But now as she modeled her clothes, she noticed curves and shapes that were not there before. Mom was always the one with the great shape. But now, in her new outfits, Cindy could see she had a body of her own, one that Bobby Wallace seemed to like.

On Monday, Cindy turned in five rough sketches of cartoons to Ms. Abbott. "Tell me which one you like," Cindy said, "and I'll finish it for the paper."

"Thanks, Cindy," Ms. Abbott said, taking the drawings. She started to laugh at the first one. "I love this one already," she said smiling. "The dough-nuts in the food machine wearing signs that say 'stale' . . . the kids'll like that. These are good too," she said, examining each of the rough pictures. "Tell you what, Cindy. Finish off the first one, and I'll hold the others for later."

Cindy was thrilled Ms. Abbott liked her work. She couldn't wait to share the news with Bobby. It seemed as if days had passed before she finally found him at lunchtime in the cafeteria.

"Bobby, you shoulda seen Ms. Abbott laughing at my drawings. She already picked one out for the next school paper," Cindy said excitedly.

"Yeah?" Bobby replied. His eyes wandered across her body. "Cindy, you look good today. How about we get together after school?"

"Sure," Cindy said, beaming. Her heart pounded in excitement at his compliment. For an instant, she felt completely happy, as if nothing could ever bother her, not Raffie, not Mom, not anything. "Where should I meet you?" she asked playfully.

"Your last class is algebra, right? So just hang around there, and I'll meet you." Bobby pointed his finger at Cindy and added, "Girl, each time I see you, you look better and better."

Cindy felt on top of the world for the rest of the day. She could not think of anything except going out with Bobby after school. She felt so beautiful in her new top and black pants. She felt as if she sparkled.

After algebra class, Cindy waited in the hall for Bobby. She felt a little foolish when Mr. Corcoran came out and noticed her standing there alone. "I'm waiting for someone," Cindy explained. After twenty minutes, Cindy began to wonder if Bobby had forgotten to meet her. But he had seemed so excited about getting together, she thought. How could he forget? Cindy glanced at her watch. Maybe she had misunderstood him. She decided to check to see if he was waiting in his car.

Cindy hurried out of the school and approached Bobby's red Nissan. The car was locked, and there was no sign he had been there. Worried that something bad happened to him, she rushed back to the hall outside the algebra classroom.

Just as she entered the hall, Cindy spotted Bobby standing against a row of lockers. His arms were crossed, and his face seemed tense.

"Bobby!" Cindy called as she came down the hall, "Where were you? I waited here for—"

"Where were *you*?" Bobby shot back, anger swirling in his dark eyes. "I told you to wait right here, didn't I? I was in the gym talking to the coach, and then I come here and you're a no-show."

"Bobby, I waited almost a half hour and then I—"

"Come on." Bobby yelled, grabbing Cindy's hand. His fingers clamped on her wrist, shooting pain up her arm. "We've wasted enough time. Next time I tell you to wait, just wait," he growled.

Bobby pulled Cindy along so fast she had to jog to keep up. She was afraid that if she stumbled, he would drag her all the way through the parking lot.

At the car, Bobby yanked open the door on the passenger side and pushed Cindy. "Get in," he said impatiently. She could see his pulse throbbing in his neck as he spoke. He seemed to be a completely different person than the one she knew. The change frightened her.

As he circled around to the driver side of the car, Cindy noticed a bruise beginning to form where he had grabbed her. Bobby sat down and started the car without a word.

"Bobby, I waited for you for a long time," Cindy explained. "I don't know why you're mad. I mean, was I supposed to stand there forever?"

"If there's one thing I can't stand, it's a girl who does something stupid and then tries to argue about it. Don't argue with me, Cindy, okay? Let's just forget about it. I said to wait, and that's what you were supposed to do. End of story," he said.

Suddenly, Bobby stomped down on the accelerator and rocketed his car through the Bluford parking lot, nearly sideswiping a Toyota Tercel that was passing by the school. Cindy looked at him in fear and confusion. Bobby seemed possessed, as if the person she knew had been replaced by some violent spirit.

The driver of the Tercel yelled, "Learn to drive!" as he passed, and Bobby's eyes narrowed with anger.

"What's his problem? He got another thing comin' if he figures he can diss me like that." Bobby raced his Nissan up along the side of the Tercel and then darted in front of it. The other driver had to slam on his brakes to avoid hitting Bobby's car.

"Bobby, what's wrong with you?" Cindy asked.

He looked over at Cindy and chuckled. "Relax, girl. That fool was askin' for it. Now I got him trapped behind me. He was in such a big hurry, but he ain't goin' nowhere now."

Bobby cut his speed to fifteen miles per hour even though the speed limit was forty. The driver of the Tercel blared his horn at Bobby, but he could not pass because of oncoming traffic. "I'll bet he's burning up," Bobby said. He smirked as he looked at the other car in the rearview mirror.

Cindy grew more nervous with each second. "Bobby, that's enough. Just drive normal, okay? Everybody is honking behind us."

"Nobody tells me when it's enough! I see the punk back there. He's goin' nuts. Man, he's having a heart attack," Bobby said with a spiteful glare.

An angry chorus of horns blared loudly from several cars, but Bobby only laughed harder. "I don't hear a thing," he said, flipping on the radio. Deep rap bass pumped through the car, shaking the back windshield.

"Please, Bobby," Cindy begged. "Just drive normal!"

"What's wrong with you? That punk dissed me, and I'm teaching him a lesson. You think I got no pride? You expect me to take static from somebody like that? Look at him. He's gonna think twice before he messes with me again."

They finally reached a cross street, and the Tercel shot out like a rocket, speeding into the intersection and nearly hitting a truck. Bobby waved mockingly at the driver as he passed.

Minutes later, they turned into the parking lot of Bobby's favorite Chinese takeout place. Almost instantly, a beat-up pickup pulled in beside them. Cindy recognized the truck's driver as he started to approach Bobby.

"Hey Wallace," Cooper Hodden, a Bluford junior and friend of Darcy Wills, shouted. "What kinda fool are you, man? I was the third car in that parade. Brotha, you are gonna get yourself shot one day if you keep that up. Of course, your head is so thick, a bullet might just bounce off," Cooper added.

"Hey, Coop," Bobby said. "Don't start lecturing me. That punk dissed me big time, and I don't take that from nobody."

"Hey, you keep actin' like that, and you're gonna end up in the morgue with a tag on your toe," Cooper said, shaking his head and returning to his pickup.

Bobby looked down at Cindy and said, "Let's go eat, Cinderella."

Inside the restaurant, Bobby ordered two orange chicken dinners. "That's what you liked before, right?" he said.

"Yeah," Cindy mumbled, dazed. She was not hungry, and despite how eager she had been to see Bobby, what she wanted most now was to go home. The driving incident had shaken her, and her wrist still throbbed with pain from Bobby's grip. As she looked at him, she did not know what to think. How could the same person who called her Cinderella act so violently?

As they waited for their chicken, Bobby said, "Have you ever seen Cooper's girlfriend, Tarah Carson? Man, I don't know what that boy sees in her. She's so big, Cooper needs that truck just to drive her around," Bobby snorted. "I'd have nightmares if I was with a girl who looked like that. But not with you, Cinderella. You're the kind of girl guys dream about. You look so good in that shirt, you gotta wear more clothes like that." As he spoke, he gently reached over and ran the back of his hand down Cindy's cheek. "When you're near me, I can't take my eyes off you."

Cindy smiled and blushed. Bobby's words were intoxicating. Instantly, they began to melt away her fear. As she and Bobby continued to talk, their argument at Bluford faded like a distant memory. Bobby would never intentionally hurt her, she thought.

"Sorry I acted a little crazy back there," he said. "I'm just having a bad day."

"It's okay, Bobby," she replied, touching his hand.

Just then a horn honked out in the parking lot. Bobby cocked his head as if he recognized a signal. It was two short blasts. "Uh-oh, that's . . . my uncle. He was gonna let me know about a job. Just sit tight. Don't go nowhere while I run out to the parking lot and see him."

Bobby spent about ten minutes outside. Cindy never saw who he was talking to, but she did see a car leaving as Bobby came back inside. It was a smoke-silver Mercedes. Cindy froze. She had seen a car like that once before in her neighborhood. The last time Raffie Whitaker came to the apartment to take her mother out, he arrived in a new car that he had just bought—a smoke-silver Mercedes. *Could it be the same car?*

"Sorry 'bout that," Bobby said, sitting down to the orange chicken. "I hope this is still warm."

"They just brought it out from the kitchen," Cindy said. She could not contain her curiosity about the Mercedes. "Bobby," she said, "is your uncle's name Raffie Whitaker?"

For a second, Cindy noticed an odd expression flash across Bobby's face, but just as quickly, it vanished. "Say what?" Bobby asked.

"The guy who dates my mom. His name is Raffie Whitaker. He drives a car like your uncle's car," Cindy said.

Bobby's eyes narrowed. "Since when did you become a detective?" he asked. "I ain't got no Uncle Raffie, so it can't be the same person." He paused briefly. "Look, Cindy, don't go spyin' on my life. All right? I don't like that. Girls always want to give me static about my friends, and I'm sick of hearing it. Just 'cause I like you don't mean you can go checking up on me like an old married lady keepin' a leash on her husband."

"Whatever," Cindy said quietly, surprised and hurt by his words. Just as quickly as he relaxed her minutes before, Bobby made her nervous again. When Bobby was nice, Cindy could not be any happier. But she had never seen this moody side of him before. And now, he seemed to be hiding something. Sitting next to him, Cindy did not know what else to say, so she brought up her cartoons again and how much Ms. Abbott liked them.

"That's nice," Bobby said. "So what time you gotta be home from school today?"

"Mom gets home around five," Cindy replied, looking at her watch. "It's already after four."

"Too bad. I was hopin' we might go

95

someplace else when we're finished here. That's all right, though. I got other things I gotta take care of," he said, watching cars pass on the street outside the restaurant.

Bobby drove Cindy home in almost complete silence. Just before he left, he grabbed her and kissed her. It was a rough, almost forceful kiss, one Cindy didn't enjoy.

Weary from the day's events, Cindy walked slowly up the stairs to her apartment. She had mixed feelings about Bobby and wanted desperately to talk to somebody. She liked Bobby, and it felt good to have a boyfriend. She especially liked wearing his varsity jacket. But she was a little nervous around him. As much as Cindy did not want to admit it, she was almost afraid of Bobby. She wondered if she was overreacting.

Cindy knew not to call Amberlynn or Jamee—they would just say, *I told you so! Drop him, girl!*

As Cindy neared her apartment, her thoughts were interrupted by the sound of Mrs. Davis's voice.

"Cindy?" the old woman called from her apartment at the end of the hall.

"Hi, Grandma Rose."

"Hello, child. I happened to be looking out the window when I saw you come home with that Wallace boy. Would you like to come over for a nice warm cup of tea?"

"Okay," Cindy said. Her mother would not be home for half an hour. Cindy was eager to talk to somebody.

She sat at Mrs. Davis's kitchen table, and after fixing some mint tea, Mrs. Davis sat opposite her. Cindy could not remember a time when she and her mother just sat together. Whenever they managed to talk, her mother was always distracted by bills, her makeup, her job, or Raffie.

"So, is this Bobby Wallace treating you right, child? Is he respecting you?"

"He's nice . . . most of the time," Cindy admitted.

"What about the rest of the time?" Mrs. Davis asked.

Cindy decided not to mention the stranger in the Mercedes or how Bobby had bruised her arm. Instead she told Mrs. Davis about the driving incident. "He was so mad at this guy that he drove real slow in front of him and held up a whole bunch of cars, and I was . . . scared," she confessed.

Harold Davis had been sitting over in the corner quietly doing his homework. Cindy barely noticed him until he piped up. "I saw that. I was walking along the street and saw eight cars held up behind Bobby's car. I thought someone was gonna jump out and strangle him for driving that way."

"That was real stupid of Bobby," Mrs. Davis said. "Somebody coulda gotten into an accident and been hurt real bad."

"I know," Cindy said sadly.

"Child, you better be careful, runnin' around with a boy like that," Mrs. Davis warned. "He could get you in a world of trouble."

"I know," Cindy repeated softly.

As she walked back to her apartment, Cindy thought about Bobby and the mysterious driver of the Mercedes. Rubbing the bruise on her arm, she wondered what had made Bobby behave so violently. Would he act that way again?

Chapter 7

Alone in the apartment, Cindy could not shake the Mercedes from her mind. *There had to be a connection between the car and Raffie*, she thought. *Who else in their neighborhood drove such an expensive car?* She could ask Mom, but her mother would probably not discuss Raffie, not after the fight they had. Cindy decided to try a new approach with Mom. She would cook dinner, something Aunt Shirley had once taught her.

By the time her mother walked in the door, Cindy had a spaghetti dinner nearly complete.

"My, what a surprise," Mom said. "You actually did some work for a change and didn't just sit around waiting for me to do everything."

Cindy stopped herself from yelling back because she did not want to start another fight. She just wanted to find out if Raffie was the driver of the Mercedes she had seen earlier that day.

"Mom," Cindy said, after her mother had a helping of spaghetti. "What kind of work does Raffie do?"

Her mother put her fork down and eyed Cindy. "What are you up to?"

"Nothing, Mom," Cindy answered.

"I've told you before he is a salesman—a darn good one too. What makes you so interested in him all of a sudden?" Cindy could see her mother was in a bad mood. Maybe something had gone wrong at work or with Raffie.

"I don't know. You said you were gonna marry him, didn't you?" Cindy said.

"If he ever gets around to asking me," she sighed.

"What's the matter? You and Raffie have a fight or something?" Cindy asked, drizzling French dressing on the salad she had prepared.

"You'd love to hear that, wouldn't you?" Mom asked, with a smirk. "Sometimes he can be such a pain. I was sure he was gonna give me a ring in Vegas. But he put it off again. I know he loves me. I mean, he's just beside himself when we don't see each other for a few days. He's crazy about me, but there's something about marriage that just seems to scare men these days."

"Mom, does Raffie have a nephew who goes to Bluford?" Cindy asked, thinking about what Bobby said about the man in the Mercedes.

Her mother looked puzzled. She twirled some spaghetti on her fork and thought for a second. Then she shook her head. "Raffie doesn't have any brothers or sisters, so he couldn't have a nephew."

"I thought I saw Raffie's car at the Chinese take-out this afternoon. Whoever it was had a smoke-silver Mercedes, and I've never seen another one of those around here."

"It couldn't have been Raffie. He's been out of town for two days. He had a sales convention in Los Angeles. He made a big presentation and everything," her mother said.

"Oh," Cindy responded, dismissing her suspicion of the strange Mercedes. *It must have just been a coincidence,* she concluded.

"What's that?" her mother asked, pointing to the bruise on Cindy's wrist.

"Nothing," Cindy answered quickly.

"I bumped myself when I was getting something out of the closet." Cindy moved her arm as she spoke so her mother would not stare at the bruise. There was no way she was going to tell her mother what Bobby did. "So, do you want some ice cream?" Cindy asked, changing the subject.

"Cindy, you know I can't eat sweets. They go right to my hips, and Lord knows they don't need to get any bigger. That reminds me, I saw your cousin Teresa today. She came into the restaurant with her boyfriend," her mother said. "She didn't look so good. If I didn't know she was twenty-four, I'd say she was about forty years old. She looks like she lost about twenty pounds. If you ask me, I think she's into drugs again too," her mother added, shaking her head. "Drugs are everywhere in this neighborhood these days. Raffie and I keep talking about leaving this place for good as soon as we get married."

Cindy thought about her mother's plan. There was no way she was going to live with her mother and Raffie. Keeping her thoughts to herself, Cindy scooped some ice cream into a bowl. She was happy to talk to her mother, even if she was not being totally honest. It felt good to see her without yelling or slamming doors. Cindy wanted to tell her what had been happening at school with Ms. Abbott and with Bobby.

"Hey, Mom, do you wanna stay here tonight and rent a movie or something?" she asked hopefully.

"I can't just sit and watch a movie," her mother replied. "I'm going over to the mall to get some new clothes. My outfits just don't fit the way they used to. When we were in Vegas, Raffie kept teasing me about it. He kept saying 'Come on, Pudge.' I wore that bare midriff outfit I bought—the one I thought I looked so good in. I just kept oozing out of it, and Raffie needled me the whole time." As she spoke, she shook her head as if to dislodge the memory.

"Raffie's mean, Mom. He's got a mean streak," Cindy insisted.

"Oh, he does not! He just likes to tease," Mom snapped.

"He has a way of figuring out what really bothers somebody, and then he shoves it in your face," Cindy said. "That's mean."

"You're not fair, Cindy. You never give Raffie a chance. He's a sweetheart. He

103

just likes to kid around, that's all," she said. "Well, I gotta go. Thanks for making dinner."

"Mom, maybe I could tag along," Cindy suggested. "We never go out together, and maybe it'd be fun if—"

"Not tonight, Cindy," her mother said. "Just rent your movie and call a friend over. See, Raffie said he'd be back tonight, and we decided to meet at that restaurant across from the mall. Since he's just getting back from the convention in L.A., I think it's best if the two of us have some quiet time together. I better get ready." She got up and hurried down the hall to change.

Cindy sat in the old recliner and watched her mother rush down the hallway. The apartment was silent except for the occasional thud of her mother opening and closing drawers in her bedroom. Cindy knew what the sounds meant; her mother was trying to find something pretty to wear for Raffie. *Everything she does anymore is for Raffie,* Cindy thought bitterly. Leaning back into the chair, Cindy wondered if her mother would be happier without her.

Cindy awoke with Theo rubbing his

furry face against her cheek. The apartment was dark, and Cindy realized she had fallen asleep in the recliner. The wall clock said it was nearly 8:00, and Cindy knew from the silence that her mother was gone. In the dark quiet of the gloomy living room, Cindy could hear noises coming from neighboring apartments. The sounds of other people talking made her feel more alone than ever.

She wondered if Mrs. Davis would mind her coming over. She thought it might seem rude to invite herself, but she did not want to spend the entire evening alone.

Cindy rang the Davises' doorbell.

"Well, hello there, honeychild," Mrs. Davis said.

"Uh, I was just sitting down to watch TV, and I can't find the *TV Guide*," Cindy lied. "I was wondering if you had one that I could borrow?"

"Come on in and watch TV with us," replied Mrs. Davis warmly, swinging the apartment door wide open. "Harold has some scary show on. Maybe you can get him to watch something a little less frightening." Mrs. Davis chuckled.

Cindy thanked her and went into the living room. She sat down on the worn sofa, next to Harold.

"Hey, Cindy," he said with a smile.

Cindy smiled back at him. The ending credits of whatever show Harold had been watching were scrolling on the small TV screen in the Davis living room. "It's over, Grandma," he yelled so she could hear him in the kitchen. "She doesn't like shows with monsters in them," Harold explained. "But I tell her there's nothin' in a fake TV show that's scarier than things in the real world." He grabbed a nearby paper plate filled with cookies and held it towards Cindy. "Try one. Grandma made them. They're real good."

Cindy took a chocolate chip cookie from the plate and ate it. Harold was right. The cookie was warm and sweet, and somehow it tasted as if it had been made with love. There was no such love in TV dinners, Cindy thought.

Mrs. Davis came into the living room then. "There's a nice show on tonight about these angels that go around performing miracles, Harold," she said. "You young people should really watch programs like that, instead of all that cussin' and killin' that they show on TV."

Harold looked at Cindy and grinned. The more she was around him, the less shy he seemed.

Mrs. Davis sighed and sat down in a big chair. She took a pile of yarn from the knitting bag next to her and dropped it on her lap. Cindy figured that as a young child, Harold had probably spent many happy hours in that lap. It seemed made for snuggling children.

Cindy reached for another cookie and noticed Harold staring at the bruise on her wrist. A strange look crossed his face, but he did not say anything.

Mrs. Davis followed his gaze for a second and then interrupted the awkward silence. "So, which classes do the two of you have together?"

"We both have English with Mr. Mitchell. And we have history together too," Harold said. "Mr. Mitchell's the nice teacher I told you about who wears the really weird clothes."

"Did you see him on Friday? He wore a red shirt and a purple tie. He looked a little like a clown," Cindy said, shaking her head. "But he's real cool. If you need to talk about something, he'll always take time to listen."

"Just don't ask him for advice on how to dress," Harold said with a smile.

"He sounds like the kind of teacher kids need. I wish there were more like him," Mrs. Davis said. "Back in my day, all the teachers took time out to sit down with students and talk, just like parents would. Nowadays, everything has changed so. It's a shame. Seems like too many teachers today just sit back and let the kids run wild."

"Cindy, didn't you say you're drawing for the *Bluford Bugler?*" Harold asked, suddenly changing the subject.

"Yeah," Cindy replied. "Why?"

"I was wondering if I could see your drawings sometime," Harold said.

"You can see them anytime," Cindy said excitedly, happy that he was interested in her work. "We can go right now if you want."

"Grandma, I'm gonna go over and see Cindy's work," Harold said. "Okay?"

"Go on, go on," Mrs. Davis laughed, waving her hand in the air. "Give me a little peace!" She chuckled to herself, the knitting needles working back and forth in her strong dark hands.

Cindy turned to Harold as soon as they stepped into the hallway. "I love your grandma," she said.

"Yeah, she's great," he said. "Sometimes I think she's a little nosy, but that's because she's always watching out for people, making sure everybody's okay. Every day, she looks out the window to keep an eye on what's going on in the neighborhood. She thinks it's her job or something."

"I wish I had someone watching over me like that," Cindy said.

"Don't worry," Harold replied. "She watches you too."

Cindy smiled. She liked the idea that someone cared about her, even if her mother didn't.

As soon as they entered the apartment, Cindy ran into her room and grabbed her scrapbook. "Some of these are old," she said, handing the book to Harold. "I've been drawing since I was a kid."

"Wow, you're really good," Harold exclaimed, leafing through the book. "I had no idea you could draw like this."

"Thanks, Harold." Cindy was excited to have someone to show her work to. When he finished looking at the sketches, Harold stood up and started to walk around the living room.

"I'm really glad you let me see your drawings," Harold said, pacing back and forth. He seemed nervous. At one point, he started to say something, but then stopped himself.

"What's wrong, Harold?" she asked.

"Uh . . . I noticed your wrist when we were at my place," he stammered. "It's pretty bruised."

"Oh, it's nothing," Cindy blurted out. "See, I was reaching for something in my closet, and I hit my wrist . . ."

Harold stared at Cindy. She could see in his eyes that he did not believe her. Cindy stopped speaking and turned away from him. She wanted to shift Harold's attention from her wrist to something else, anything else.

"You're goin' out with Bobby Wallace now, aren't you?" Harold asked.

"Yeah," she admitted reluctantly, afraid of what Harold would say next.

"When Jamee went out with Bobby, she had bruises like that," Harold said, pointing to her wrist.

"Oh, I get it. So now you're going to be like everybody else and tell me to stay away from him, right?" Cindy replied.

Harold paused briefly as if he was searching for the right words. "Cindy, that kid is no good. He don't bring girls anything but trouble. When I was in middle school with Jamee, I'd see her going with him," he continued. "She was only in eighth grade, and he was a junior at Bluford."

"Harold, I know what you're trying to say, but Bobby didn't mean to hurt me. He's just strong, that's all," she explained.

"If I were you," Harold replied, "I'd—"

"But you aren't me, Harold!" Cindy yelled. "This really isn't any of your business. Everyone keeps telling me what I should do, but no one ever asks how I feel or what I want, not you, not Jamee, not Mom. You don't know me, Harold. Right now, Bobby is the best thing I got, better than school, better than this nasty apartment, better than anything."

Cindy could see that her words stunned Harold. For a second, he did not say anything. Then he looked at her. "I'm sorry, Cindy. I just don't want to see anything bad happen to you, that's all."

"I appreciate that, Harold, but Bobby's been really nice to me. He's even letting me wear his football jacket. Honest, he's nice," Cindy said, unsure whether she believed what she was saying.

Harold took a long breath. "Well, if you ever want to talk to someone," he said, "I'm only down the hall."

"Thanks," Cindy said, hoping he was not going to pressure her any further. "I'm sorry I snapped at you, Harold. You're really nice."

"It's okay, I asked for it," he said, looking around the room as if he wanted to change the subject. His gaze stopped at the clown sculpture on the coffee table. "What's that?" he asked.

"Isn't that the ugliest thing you ever saw? Raffie got it for Mom. I bet he got it at a junkyard for fifty cents or something, but Mom acts like it's some wonderful expensive masterpiece 'cause it's from him," Cindy said.

Harold picked up the clown sculpture for a closer look. "Who did you say bought this?"

"Raffie Whitaker, my mom's boyfriend. He's always buying her ugly stuff."

Harold looked at Cindy as if she had just insulted him. Without saying a word, he stepped back and placed the clown back on top of the coffee table, shaking his head.

"Harold, what's wrong?"

"Raffie Whitaker. Is he *really* your mom's boyfriend?"

"Yeah, do you know him?" Cindy asked.

"I know *of* him," Harold said. "He's a drug dealer."

Chapter 8

Harold's words cracked through the room like a thunderclap. Cindy felt as though the living-room floor shifted beneath her feet, as if the whole world had somehow lost its balance.

"What?" Cindy gasped.

"I thought you knew. How else do you think he pays for everything?" Harold asked with widened eyes. "I don't mean to be rude, but what's your mother see in a guy like that?" Harold inquired. "She seems like a pretty sharp lady."

Cindy didn't want to talk anymore. She closed her eyes tightly, trying to block out the images she was seeing in her mind. Raffie and Mom together in a drug bust. Mom using drugs again. It was all too painful to think about. "Look, Harold, I've got homework to do, and I have to do a sketch for—"

"I'm sorry if I upset you, Cindy," Harold said, putting his hand on her shoulder. "Do you wanna work at my grandma's place?"

"No," Cindy replied. "I just need to be by myself for a while. Tell your grandma that I'm sorry, but I just wanna stay here."

"Okay, well, I guess I'll see you later," Harold said, hurrying to leave.

Back in her apartment, Cindy thought about what Harold had said. Even though she had no real proof, Cindy knew his words were true. Since the day she met Raffie, she had not trusted him, sensing all along that he was secretive and dishonest. What disturbed her most was not that Raffie was selling drugs, but that Mom was still planning to marry him. Cindy was not sure whether her mother knew the truth about Raffie, but she knew she had to confront her as soon as possible. She decided to wait on the couch until her mother came home.

It was close to midnight when Cindy heard her mother's keys jingling against the apartment door.

"Cindy," Mom grumbled as she walked in, "tomorrow's a school day.

Why are you still up?"

"Mom, I gotta talk to you," Cindy said. "It's really important."

"Now what?" her mother groaned. "I've already had a bad day—rude customers, Raffie not showing up at the restaurant. Now I gotta hear one of your problems!"

Cindy swallowed hard. "Mom, Raffie is a drug dealer."

Cindy's mother dropped her coat and glared at her daughter. "Girl, shut your mouth! You want me to slap you? How dare you say such a thing! I can't believe you're so jealous of him that you'd make up lies like this."

"Mom!" Cindy cried desperately.

"I'm sick of hearing you talk bad about Raffie!" Mom yelled. "Now you're makin' up lies about him. This has got to stop. It just has to stop!"

"A guy from school told me everybody knows Raffie's a dealer," Cindy explained.

"Well, everybody is wrong! People are always spreading rumors about Raffie because they are jealous of how successful he is. Raffie's a good man, Cindy. Don't you spread lies about him, and don't you ever repeat to me the garbage you hear! Understand?"

"Mom!" Cindy pleaded, tears in her eyes. "It's the truth."

"I don't want to hear another word about it! Understand? I'm tired, and I'm going to bed!" She hurried down the hall and slammed her bedroom door.

Tears were streaming down Cindy's cheeks by the time she reached her bedroom. She crawled into bed and buried her head in her pillow. It was just a matter of time, Cindy thought, before Raffie would get someone arrested or killed. Maybe it would be Mom.

Frightened, Cindy trembled in her dark bedroom for hours, the silence interrupted occasionally by the distant howl of a far-away police siren.

The next morning, Cindy and Mom exchanged no words at breakfast. Cindy could tell her mother was still bitter about the previous night's discussion. The tension in the small kitchen was so thick that Cindy was glad to sling on her backpack and get out of the apartment, even if she was going to Bluford.

On the way to school, Cindy wondered what she should do. Her mother would not listen to her, and she could think of no one who could help her. Then, as she approached Bluford, Cindy saw Bobby arriving at school in his Nissan. Maybe he would be able to help, she thought. Yet as she walked up to his car, she thought of him leaving the Chinese restaurant to talk to the mysterious man in the Mercedes. *Was there a connection?* she wondered.

"Hey, Bobby," she said quickly. "Listen, I have something important to tell you. I found out that Raffie Whitaker, the guy my mom is dating, is a drug dealer! I'm so scared."

Bobby sat there a moment, expressionless, and then slowly got out of the car. His silent reaction made her even more desperate. She knew he was hiding something from her.

"That was Raffie you were talking to in the parking lot the other day, wasn't it?" Cindy, asked, tears in her eyes. "Bobby, why'd you lie to me? You're not into drugs, are you?"

"Cinderella, relax," he said gently, putting his hand softly on her back. "I told you, I was strung out last year, but that's ancient history. I'm clean now, I swear it. There's no way I'm going down that road again."

"I'm glad," Cindy said, relieved. "But what did Raffie want with you?"

"He heard about how I was last year and wondered if I'd find him some punks to buy this new stuff he's selling. It's a drug they use to put cats to sleep. Whitaker says it's a real trip. I told him to get lost. That's all it was." Bobby smiled at Cindy and wrapped his arms around her gently. "You ain't got a worry in the world about your man, Cinderella," he insisted.

Cindy was grateful to hear Bobby's words. She needed someone to talk to, someone to trust, and Bobby seemed to understand that. Enveloped in his arms, she felt safe. This was the side of Bobby that Harold did not know about, she thought. Cindy put her arms on Bobby's back and pulled him closer. For a second, buried in Bobby's arms, she did not worry about anything. Then thoughts of her mother flooded her mind. "Bobby, I'm so scared Raffie will get my mom in trouble."

"Listen, I'll see what I can do. Just don't talk to nobody else about this, okay? Stay cool," Bobby said. "I'll take care of business."

"What are you gonna do?"

"I'll figure something out. Trust me," he assured her. "Now guess what," he said, winking. "I got something for you."

"Yeah?" Cindy asked, her heart racing.

"Meet me after school at my car."

"I will, Bobby," Cindy promised, grateful that he was going to help her though still unsure about his connection to Raffie.

At lunchtime, Cindy noticed some seniors gathered in the schoolyard. Bobby was among them. Next to him were André Watkins and Pedro Ortiz. They had reputations as troublemakers and druggies. Cindy watched uneasily from the other side of the schoolyard as Bobby talked. She wondered what he was saying. Perhaps he was warning the other kids about Raffie and his new drug. If Raffie's Bluford customers drifted away, Cindy thought, then maybe he would go somewhere else and leave her mother alone.

After classes, Cindy went to turn in her finished cartoon to Ms. Abbott.

"Excellent work, Cindy. You are very talented," the teacher said. "We've all been very impressed with what you've done so far. You should be very proud of yourself."

"Thanks," said Cindy, smiling.

"There's a national drawing contest that I just heard about today," Ms. Abbott continued, "and I thought that maybe you might like to enter it. You're certainly good enough. Top prize is five hundred dollars."

"That sounds great," Cindy said, trying to sound excited. She was honored that Ms. Abbott mentioned the contest to her, but she was unable to think of anything except her mother, Raffie, and Bobby.

"Well, I'll get you all the information." The teacher smiled. "We can fill out the paperwork together. Just gather your best work to enter."

Cindy thanked Ms. Abbott quickly and left, explaining that she had another meeting to go to. The truth was that she was worried about her mother and eager to talk to Bobby.

Cindy made it to the Nissan before Bobby did. As she waited for him, she saw a smoke-silver Mercedes cruising down the street and then stop near the school parking lot. Looking closely, she recognized the driver—it was Raffie. An attractive female student from Bluford ran to the car, and Raffie smiled and talked to her. Cindy shuddered. She wondered what Mom would say if she were watching him now.

As Cindy waited for Bobby, Pedro Ortiz stepped out of Bluford and swaggered into the parking lot towards her. He was wearing a baseball cap sideways on his head, and his hands were stuffed into the pockets of black oversized jeans. A ratty black leather jacket with a Raiders logo hung on his broad shoulders. As he walked past Cindy, he fixed his eyes on her. She felt uncomfortable in his gaze.

"Don't get in over your head," he said mysteriously as he passed.

"What are you talking about?" she asked. Pedro did not answer. Instead, he continued walking casually towards the Mercedes. As he neared the end of the parking lot, the Mercedes cruised away. Pedro stopped where he was and mumbled something under his breath. Then he turned and headed back towards school.

Bobby came along as Pedro was walking away. The two boys nodded but didn't say a word. When Bobby reached

Cindy, she said, "That guy gives me the creeps."

"Pedro? He's cool. He's just a homey, Cinderella," Bobby said.

"He on drugs too?" Cindy asked.

Bobby smiled. "Girl, you've got to calm down. Just go with the flow."

Cindy was not satisfied with that answer. How could she relax when her mother wanted to marry a drug dealer who cruised the local high school? Frustrated, she plopped down in the Nissan. "Where are we going?"

"Down to the ocean, baby," he said. "We're gonna park and walk down on the sand. It might do you some good to get away for a little while. You need a break."

Despite her anxiety about her mother, Cindy liked Bobby's idea. It was only 3:00, so they had plenty of time to go and come back before it got late. Besides, Cindy thought, even if she wanted to talk to her mother again, she would have to wait a few hours for her to come home from work. She'd rather be with Bobby at the beach than alone in the empty apartment.

"Let's go!" she said excitedly.

When they got to the beach, Bobby spread a huge towel on the sand. It was a cool day, and there were few people around. Cindy sat on the towel, with Bobby's arm around her, watching the waves roll in from the horizon.

"It's so pretty here," Cindy said, listening to the rhythmic crashing of the waves. "I'd love to have a house right here. I'd wake up to the sun shining off the ocean, and go to sleep listening to the sound of waves."

"Who knows," Bobby said. "Maybe someday I'll be rich. Who says it can't happen? Coach says I could go pro after college. First thing I'd do is build you a house on the beach, no matter how much it cost."

"Bobby," Cindy said, shaking her head. She couldn't believe he was talking about their future. She liked the thought of them still being together in the days to come. But as she thought about the future, her mind drifted back towards her mother. What would the future bring for her? Cindy wondered.

Cindy wrapped her arms around her knees and looked out over the crimsoned water. The sun was beginning to set. "It's getting late," she said sadly. "I'd better be getting home soon."

Bobby reached in his pocket and

123

handed her a small wrapped box. "Here's the surprise I promised you," he said.

"Bobby," Cindy exclaimed, "what did you buy?"

She had never received a gift from a boy. Her hands trembled as she fumbled with the ribbon and opened the box. A golden bracelet sparkled in the dimming sunlight. "A bracelet! Oh, it's beautiful," Cindy cried, pulling it out of the box. "I've never owned anything as nice as this," she said. It was so rich looking, so delicate with three little charms hanging on it. One was a heart, the second an arrow, and then a tiny letter "B".

Cindy's hands were trembling so much she could not put the bracelet on. Bobby reached over gently. "Here, let me help."

"I can't believe you got this for me, Cindy said, "I'm so happy I could die!"

"You don't wanna do that!" he laughed, delighted by her reaction.

It was 6:30 when Bobby finally dropped Cindy off at home. Before she left his car, she gave him a long kiss. It was their nicest one so far, and her heart raced with excitement.

When Cindy stepped out of the car,

she felt so happy that she almost forgot her problems with her mother. But as she approached the apartment, her worries came rushing back. What should she say to her mother about Raffie?

Cindy slowly opened the front door, hoping her mother would be in a good mood.

"Hey Ugly Mugly," said a familiar voice. It was Raffie sitting on the living-room sofa. "You lookin' for a bag for that face?" he sneered.

Cindy heard her mother rattling dishes in the kitchen. She was unable to hear anything Raffie said.

Instantly, Cindy's pulse started to throb, and her palms began to sweat. She wanted to call the police or somehow force her mother to see the truth about Raffie. Yet Cindy knew she had no proof, and her mother would not listen to her. For a moment, the two stared at each other in icy silence.

"Whatcha gonna do, Ugly Mugly?" Raffie challenged.

As she looked into his cold dark eyes, Cindy's anger grew. Sitting on her couch was a man who had insulted her, lied to her mother, and risked destroying their fragile family.

"I know you're a drug dealer," Cindy said in a low, angry rasp. "I don't care what happens to you, but you better not get my mom in trouble," she warned.

"Whoa, you got some mouth on you, girl," Raffie said, twirling one of the gold chains around his neck. "You best watch that mouth, or you might be picking your teeth out of your lap. You get my meaning?"

Just then Cindy's mother came in with a plate of cold shrimp and crackers, Raffie's favorite snack. "Hey, Cindy," her mother said. "Why don't you have some shrimp with Raffie and me."

Cindy did not even acknowledge her mother. She glared quickly at Raffie, rushed into her bedroom, and slammed the door so hard the walls trembled.

From her room, Cindy heard her mother laugh nervously and try to smooth over Cindy's behavior. "Oh, Raffie, she's just being a teenager, that's all. I swear sometimes I think all mothers should get a warning about how their adorable babies can turn into teenage monsters!"

Raffie chuckled. "She's just going through some growing pains right now. She'll get used to me," he assured her.

"She don't have any other choice," he added.

"That's right, baby," her mother said. "That's right."

Cindy flopped onto her bed and stared at the ceiling. She felt as if she was locked in a jail cell, one which she would never escape.

Chapter 9

The next day, Cindy decided she had to talk to someone about Raffie. Instead of going home after school, she went directly to Mrs. Davis's apartment. Harold was not home yet when she arrived. Mrs. Davis answered the door and brought Cindy to the kitchen.

"Sit down, honeychild, and help me wait for this pumpkin pie to finish baking," Mrs. Davis said. The rich, sweet scent of the pie filled the apartment and the outside hallway with a heavenly fragrance. Cindy sat down nervously and took a deep breath.

"Cindy," Mrs. Davis said with a warm smile. "What's wrong?"

"Grandma Rose," Cindy groaned, "this guy my mom is dating, Raffie Whitaker, he's a drug dealer. I told Mom, but she won't believe me. I'm so scared."

Mrs. Davis shook her head sadly. "Child, that Whitaker's been dealing drugs in this neighborhood for a long time. From what I hear, he's got school kids working for him. I told the police months ago. The sergeant I spoke to wrote down everything I said. He was a nice man, but nothing happened. I pray to God somebody stops Raffie Whitaker before he puts some child in an early grave."

Cindy noticed Mrs. Davis looking at her new bracelet.

"It's from Bobby," she said. "He's the only person besides you and Harold who I can talk to about all this. He's been really nice."

"Well, I'm mighty glad to hear that. I know his momma. Tina Wallace is a good woman who has had a lot of grief in her life. She's been through fire and ice with that husband of hers. Now she's tending him like a saint 'cause he's laid up with lung trouble. Bobby has been nothing but pain to her, and I hope to heaven he's turned himself around," Mrs. Davis said.

Just then, Harold came home and walked into the kitchen. "Hi, Cindy," he said, glancing quickly at his grandmother and Cindy. "I can leave if it's a bad time," he added, turning to walk out.

"It's okay," Cindy assured him. "We're just talking, that's all."

Harold hesitated briefly and asked, "Wanna go down to the library with me?"

"Sure," Cindy said, eager for any reason not to go home.

"You know that project in Mitchell's class where we gotta pick somebody who overcame great odds to become a success?" Harold asked as they headed for the library. "You pick anybody yet?"

"Yeah. I picked Ray Charles. He was blind when he was a little boy, and he was poor and lost his mother too," Cindy said. "And look what a big music career he has."

"Maybe you can help me find somebody, Cindy. I need a better grade this marking period. Grandma keeps getting on my case," Harold said.

"Well, you're talking to the wrong person," Cindy said with a laugh. "I'm not a perfect student either, but I'll try to help out."

As they approached the library, Cindy noticed Pedro Ortiz standing in a parking lot behind a grocery store.

"Look, there's Pedro. I can't stand him, Harold. I bet he's waiting to buy drugs from Raffie," Cindy said.

"Let's cross over to the other side of the street," Harold said cautiously. "We don't want to get mixed up in anything he's involved in."

"That's right," Pedro called out to them as they crossed the street. "Just keep walkin'."

"Maybe if I brought Mom down here," Cindy said, "she would believe what I've been saying about Raffie."

"Wouldn't do no good," Harold said. "She loves him, right?"

"I guess," Cindy sighed.

"Grandma says if love settles on a garbage can, you can't make the fool in love smell the stink."

In the library, Cindy and Harold searched through the aisles, stopping at the section with biographies. Cindy found a book about Franklin Roosevelt. The book focused on how he overcame his disability. "Look, this man was crippled, and he still became president," Cindy said.

"No way," Harold said. "No president of the United States was ever crippled."

"Sure he was. It's all here in the book. He had polio, and after that he never could stand up or walk unless somebody helped him."

They checked out the book on Roosevelt and headed home. "Look, Cindy," Harold said nervously. "I've been wanting to ask you something for a while, but. . . ." He hesitated and took a deep breath. "Wanna go to the movies with me on Saturday?"

Cindy smiled, flattered that Harold wanted to take her out. She had never considered him as someone she would go out with. He was her neighbor and a friend, but until now she had thought of him as nothing more. And, of course, there was Bobby. She would never go out with Harold while things were so good with Bobby. She struggled to find an answer that wouldn't hurt his feelings.

"I'd go with you in a minute, Harold. You're really nice . . . but me and Bobby are together," Cindy said.

"I understand," Harold said quietly, his eyes focused on the ground. "Just be careful," he added.

"Look, I know you don't like Bobby, but he's been good to me. Can't you just be my friend and be happy for me?" Cindy said, tired of having to defend her boyfriend.

"What about that bruise on your wrist?" Harold replied.

132

"I told you before, that was just an accident," Cindy insisted, pushing her new bracelet over the bruise.

"You're a lot like your mom, Cindy. You only see what you want to see," Harold said.

Cindy glared at Harold. She resented his comment, but she did not want to get into a fight with him. Instead, she kept quiet, and the two walked back home in awkward silence, careful to avoid the parking lot where they had seen Pedro.

Cindy's mother was in the kitchen making a casserole when Cindy came home from the library. "So where have you been? You're never home anymore," her mother said.

"I was in the library helping someone with a project," Cindy answered, wondering if her mother realized how silly such an accusation sounded coming from her. *I'm always home, Mom. You're the one who's never here*, Cindy thought.

The casserole smelled good. Her mother was a good cook when she tried, which was not often. For a terrible moment Cindy wondered if Raffie was in the apartment somewhere ready to pop out, jingling his flashy gold chains.

"You're home alone tonight, Mom?" Cindy asked.

"Yeah," she said. "Raffie had a change in plans. He was sent to Los Angeles again to cover a sales convention because someone else got sick. He's making an important presentation at this meeting in a big hotel. I don't know how he does it. How he faces all those people and gives them a sales pitch with slides and spreadsheets and everything."

"You should go with him sometime, and see how he does it," Cindy mocked. "Unless maybe he wouldn't like that."

"Skip the comments, Cindy," her mother snapped. "I know you hate Raffie, but that's your problem. You're just going to have to accept that he's my man, and soon he's going to be my husband." As she spoke, she raised her left hand. A sparkling gold ring with a large diamond glistened on her finger. "Next year, you gonna have yourself a stepfather."

"What?!" Cindy gasped.

"Raffie proposed last night and said we would get married sometime next year," her mother said with a big smile.

Cindy stared at the ring in disbelief. Her knees felt as if they were about to buckle, and twisted thoughts tumbled through her mind. For an instant, she imagined introducing Raffie to her teachers. *"This is my stepfather, the drug dealer."*

"Why . . . why are you gonna do that, Mom?" Cindy asked, her voice desperate and broken.

"Oh, for once be happy for me, Cindy," her mother chided. "I'm getting old. You don't know what it's like to be my age and not settled down yet. I don't want to be old and alone."

"Mom!" Cindy moaned in frustration. "You're not alone . . . you have me." But as she spoke, Cindy knew her words would not be enough to change her mother's mind.

Mom turned and faced her daughter. Cindy could see her mother was touched by what she had said. "Cindy, this isn't only about me. It's also for *you.* You deserve a man around the house, and who knows, maybe with Raffie's money we can send you to college. You'd be the first in our family to go," she said.

"I don't want Raffie's money or his help," Cindy insisted. "He's a drug dealer, Mom. I'm sure of it."

"Don't start that talk around me, girl. Especially not now. You're *not* going to ruin

135

this for me, Cindy. I won't let you!" she growled and stormed out of the kitchen.

Angered and saddened, Cindy went to her bedroom. As the dismal evening wore on, Cindy drew a series of sketches showing Bluford surrounded by monsters who preyed on kids. The creatures were on the streets, hanging on corners, and their faces vaguely resembled Raffie and Pedro. One victim, a girl caught in the clutches of a twisted figure, had Cindy's face.

When Cindy arrived at school Thursday morning, Bobby was waiting for her.

"Wassup, Cinderella," he said, throwing his arm around her and giving her a kiss in the middle of the crowded hallway.

"Hi," she said with a smile, unprepared for his sudden affection.

"We're goin' out tomorrow night," Bobby said. "It's Halloween, so we gotta do something together."

"Okay," Cindy replied, shrugging her shoulders. With all the distraction at home, she had forgotten about the holiday. "You know Jamee and Darcy invited me to a party at their house. They're gonna watch—"

"We ain't goin' there," Bobby interjected. "A bunch of people I know are heading to that club, the Dungeon. There's gonna be a band, and everyone's gonna get dressed up. I want to go there and show you off. Here take this," he said, handing her two fifty dollar bills.

"Bobby, why are you giving me all this money?"

"Go to the mall and get yourself a nice costume, you know, something kinda sexy. And don't be afraid to show your body. You look great. Brothas are gonna drool when they see you."

"I can't take this. It's too much!"

"Come on, Cindy. Don't worry about the money. You're my girl, and I want you to look good."

"But it's a lot of money, Bobby, and I'm not gonna be able to pay it back."

"Girl, this ain't no loan! It's a *gift*. Just get yourself something nice and come to the party with me. That's all the payback I need," he insisted.

Cindy blushed. No one had ever showed her such attention. Looking into Bobby's intense, dark eyes, she could not refuse his request.

"Okay," she said, putting the money in her pocket. "I'll find something nice to wear."

After school, Cindy took a bus to the mall with Jamee. She didn't tell her about the money from Bobby. "Mom let me have some money to buy a costume for a party tomorrow night," Cindy lied.

"I hope it's not that Dungeon party everyone's talkin' about," Jamee said.

"What do you know about it?" Cindy asked.

"I know that hoodlums hang out there," Jamee replied. "Bobby took me there once last year. The place was full of people drinking, getting high, and fighting. I wanted no part of that."

Cindy shuddered. She had never actually seen the Dungeon. And from Jamee's description, she didn't want to.

"Why don't you just come over to my house tomorrow night," Jamee said, tugging on Cindy's arm. "My sister's friends are cool. We'll have a good time."

"Jamee, I can't. I told Bobby I'd go with him. Besides, I've never done anything like this before. Maybe it'll be fun. I promise I won't do anything stupid," Cindy said. "I promise."

Jamee rolled her eyes but didn't say a word.

"Come on," Cindy added. "Let's find me a costume like we came here to do."

The girls went into a shop that carried a large variety of Halloween costumes. Cindy found a genie costume and accessories to go with it. "Oh, this is hot!" she exclaimed.

"I love it, Cindy," Jamee said.

When Cindy put the costume on, Jamee let out a howl of approval. "Damn, girl, you look good. You're going to have to fight off guys if you wear that."

"Thanks," Cindy said. She had never worn such a revealing outfit. The genie costume came in two parts, similar to a two-piece bathing suit, but with sheer fabric covering her legs. When she put it on, her entire stomach was exposed. Though she felt self-conscious, she couldn't help admiring how sexy she looked. While Jamee was distracted at a sales rack, Cindy quickly bought the costume. It was eighty dollars. Jamee would never have believed Cindy got that kind of money from her mother.

It was dusk by the time the bus returned to the neighborhood. As it lumbered past Bluford High School, Cindy spotted Pedro outside talking to a group of kids.

"Look, there's Pedro," Cindy said. "I can't stand him."

"He scares me," Jamee said, shuddering. "Darcy says he's flunking most of his classes."

"You think he's selling?" Cindy asked.

"Somebody is. The freshmen are getting all they want," Jamee said. "My sister says this is the worst she's ever seen Bluford. I heard they might bring in those drug-sniffing dogs again."

"I wish they didn't have to make our school into a prison just to keep it safe," Cindy said. "But I don't know what else they can do."

On Friday night, Cindy waited eagerly for Bobby. As soon as she spotted his red Nissan pulling up, she took one last look at herself in the snug costume and then jotted a brief note for her mother.

Mom, I'm out with friends. Be back after midnight.

Since Mom announced her engagement, Cindy had barely spoken to her. *There's no point talking if no one's listening,* Cindy thought as she taped the note to the refrigerator and ran out the door, pushing Raffie out of her mind.

"Girl, you look *good!*" Bobby exclaimed as Cindy slipped into his car. He was dressed like a pirate with a cape, eye patch, and black hat with a skull and crossbones. "You look like you just stepped off a magazine cover!" he added.

"Thanks," Cindy said, delighted at his reaction. Bobby's approval was intoxicating, and for an instant, Cindy forgot all her problems at home. For once, she was attractive and loved. She hugged Bobby warmly. "I'm glad you like the costume," she said.

"Cinderella, I like what's *in* the costume even more! I already know my three wishes, but I'll ask for them later," he joked, hugging her tightly.

"Are you sure it's safe at the Dungeon?" Cindy asked, gently pulling away from Bobby.

"Of course it is," Bobby said, steering the car into the street. "You're with me."

Cindy wanted his words to reassure her, but as she left her neighborhood, she grew more nervous.

Bobby pulled the car into a crowded parking lot and looked over at Cindy. "I can't wait to show you off," he said with a grin.

Cindy took a deep breath, trying to remain calm. "I heard this place can get

141

kinda wild," she said, hoping he would change his mind about going in.

"Relax, Cinderella. This is the Halloween jam. It's just a big party, that's all. Lots of people from Bluford and Lincoln will be there. No one will mess with you as long as I'm around. Let's go." Bobby got out of the car quickly and opened the door for Cindy. Reluctantly, she stepped out into the cool night.

In the parking lot, Cindy felt deep hip-hop bass pulsing through the air. As they neared the Dungeon, Bobby spotted a familiar vehicle parked across the street. "That's Cooper Hodden's pickup. What is that fool doin' here?" he asked.

"I don't know," Cindy replied, remembering that Cooper was supposed to be at Jamee's party. Just then, Cindy heard a voice calling her name.

"Cindy! Come here."

Cindy turned to see Jamee and Darcy standing amidst a crowd walking towards the club. Cooper Hodden and a heavy-set girl stood behind the two sisters.

"Jamee, what're you doin' here?" Cindy asked. "I thought you were having a party."

"Cindy, we're here for you. Don't go in

142

there. Just come with us," Jamee said.

"Girl, what's your problem?" Bobby growled. "Are you jealous of me and Cinderella?"

"I'm not jealous, Bobby. I just don't want my friend getting into trouble!" Jamee yelled back.

"Come on, girl," Cooper added. "Jamee's right. This place is bad news."

"Step off, Coop!" Bobby said. "This ain't got nothin' to do with you."

"Cindy, just come with us," Jamee insisted.

Cindy hesitated. She was embarrassed at the scene she was causing and unsure what to do. Jamee was serious. The determined look on her face told Cindy that she really meant what she said. Jamee cared so much that she even brought her sister and friends to help her. But then there was Bobby.

"Come on, Cindy," he said tugging at her arm. "We don't need to listen to this." Reluctantly Cindy stepped forward, looking back at the group of people who came for her. Part of her wanted to walk away from Bobby, but another part was willing to follow him almost anywhere.

"Sorry, guys," she said, turning towards the dark wooden doors.

Inside the Dungeon, they entered a strange world of flashing strobe lights, swirling smoke clouds, and throbbing music. Amidst the dense crowd, Cindy saw dozens of people dressed as goblins, movie villains, celebrities, and monsters. She felt a mixture of awe and terror in the dark and unfamiliar room. She was suddenly aware of strangers looking at her body, and she felt overly exposed in her scant genie costume.

"Bobby, how long are we staying here?" Cindy asked, crossing her arms on her chest.

"Relax, Cinderella," he replied. "The party's just getting started."

Chapter 10

Marijuana smoke hung heavy and thick in the stuffy air of the Dungeon. Cindy saw several unmasked Bluford students circling around the crowded dance floor. In the distance, she noticed a corridor which appeared to lead to another large room lined with tables.

"I just wanna let some people know I'm here. I'll be right back," Bobby said, heading towards the hallway. Before Cindy could protest, he darted into the crowd.

Alone and uncomfortable, Cindy leaned against a wall on the edge of the dance floor. She wished she and Bobby could just leave, that they could watch movies with Jamee and Darcy.

At a nearby table, she saw Dillon Baker from her English class. His glassy blue eyes bulged unnaturally from his otherwise expressionless face. He did not seem to notice her, or anything else for that matter. Suddenly, she felt a tap her shoulder.

"If you want anything, girl, I'll get it for you," a voice said. She turned and faced a guy wearing a wolf mask. As he spoke, she noticed his eyes moving up and down her body.

"No thanks," she said, crossing her arms on her chest. She felt naked and embarrassed in his gaze. "I'm here with someone," she added, hoping he would find someone else to stare at.

"I don't see anyone with you—"

"Man, get away from my girl," Bobby said, coming up behind the stranger.

"It's cool, it's cool," the guy repeated, backing into the crowd.

Bobby smiled. "You see how good you look, Cinderella? Guys are checkin' you out."

Cindy hugged Bobby gratefully. She was glad he arrived when he did, but she still wanted to leave. Looking over at Dillon Baker, Cindy felt sick. In Mr. Mitchell's class, Dillon was a nice guy and a good student. Now, he was spaced out. As she watched, a couple of his friends sat down next to him. He looked as though he barely recognized them. Cindy turned to Bobby, "I wish we could just go somewhere else, Bobby. This place bothers me."

"Just 'cause some fool hit on you?" Bobby asked with an edge to his voice. "That kid's got nothin' to do with us, Cinderella. Don't let it ruin the party. Come on, let's dance."

"Bobby, everybody here is high," Cindy said, "I just wish—"

"Girl, I want to show you off!" he demanded. His eyes narrowed as he talked. "I want the homies to see my girl."

"But—"

"Girl, drop it!" he yelled, his nostrils flaring. "Man, if there's one thing I can't stand, it's a girl who steps out with me and takes my money but then tries to stop me when I wanna do something. It's all cool when they're getting bracelets and clothes, but ask a favor and they start giving static." As Bobby spoke, his grip on Cindy's hand grew even tighter.

"Bobby, you're hurting me," Cindy said.

"Don't push me, girl. It's gonna be your fault if you get me mad and I do something stupid," Bobby warned. Then he dropped her hand as if it were an object that disgusted him and shouldered past her, knocking her into the corner of a nearby booth. Pain shot into her leg.

"You stay right here. I gotta use the bathroom. Don't move, hear?" Bobby said.

Cindy nodded. As he disappeared in the crowd, she looked at the door. She wished she could just go home, but she knew better than to walk home alone at night in her revealing costume. Maybe she could catch a bus, she thought.

Carefully, Cindy inched towards the door. She was stopped by another kid she did not know who tried to make her dance with him. His face was wrapped in bandages like a mummy. "C'mon girl, I know you know how to move," he said, grinding into her. By the time she got past him, Bobby returned. She was afraid to tell him she was trying to leave.

"I told you to wait right here," Bobby yelled. "What—are you stupid or something?"

Angered and hurt by his words, Cindy turned towards Bobby and noticed he looked different. He was sweating profusely, and his eyes were wide and glassy, like Dillon's. Cindy had seen the same look on Bobby's face the day he bruised her wrist at Bluford. Illuminated in the flashing light, he looked like a monstrous version of himself, like the figures in her drawings.

"I don't feel good . . . I need to go home," Cindy stammered, afraid to provoke him.

"Why are you messin' with me?" Bobby screamed, grabbing her shoulders. Strobe lights flashed over his head like lightning from an approaching storm.

Watching in wide-eyed terror, Cindy was flooded with an awful realization—*drugs. Bobby must be using drugs.* He had probably just used them in the bathroom. That explained his strange appearance and his violent mood swings. The power of that realization set off a chain reaction in Cindy's mind.

Bobby had been lying. He'd been lying to her since the moment they first went out together, she realized. But worse, Cindy understood, was an even bigger lie—the one she had told herself. Jamee, Mrs. Davis, and Harold had been right all along. Bobby was trouble, and she had refused to listen.

"Bobby," Cindy yelled, staring into his twitching eyes, "let me go!" Bobby shifted his hands to her neck, and his grip began to tighten around her throat. "You just never listen," he growled.

"Bobby . . . ," she gasped, unable to breathe.

Suddenly, Cindy heard a familiar voice.

"Get off her!"

Cindy glanced back to see Jamee rushing up next to her. In a blur, Jamee shoved Bobby, causing him to lose his grip on Cindy's neck. Just as quickly, Darcy, Cooper, and Tarah were next to her.

"You all right?" Darcy asked, putting her arm around Cindy.

"I'm okay," Cindy said, rubbing her neck. "I just wanna go home."

"That's why we came back," Jamee said. "There was no way we were gonna leave you here with him. I don't care what he says."

Cindy turned towards Bobby. He shook his head and clumsily approached Jamee. "I told you to stay out of this," Bobby said in a low, angry rasp. "Cindy's stayin' right here with me." His voice became hoarser with each word.

"No, Bobby. I'm going home now," Cindy yelled, wondering what Bobby had taken in the bathroom. Maybe it was that new drug Raffie was pushing. Whatever it was, it was seriously affecting Bobby. He was unsteady, and his speech was slurred.

"Yeah, back off, Wallace," Cooper warned, stepping in between Jamee and Bobby. "You ain't gonna hit any girls tonight." But as Cooper spoke, his expression changed from anger to concern. "Hey, homey, you lookin' bad—"

As they watched, Bobby grabbed for a chair and then collapsed. The saliva that had been running from his mouth turned to vomit. Somebody screamed, and a number of people panicked.

"I'm calling 911!" Darcy said, rushing to find a phone. Frightened kids began scrambling out the large front doors. Someone flicked on a light switch and the entire room brightened.

By the time the paramedics arrived, most of the kids had left the Dungeon. Cindy sat with Jamee, Darcy, Cooper, and Tarah, watching the medics put Bobby on a stretcher. He was unconscious, and Cindy could see the whites of his eyes peeking beneath his eyelids. Cindy gazed in shock at his body and the flashing red lights of the ambulance.

"What happened here?" a paramedic asked.

"A Halloween party gone bad, real bad," Darcy replied.

The emergency technician shook his head and slammed the doors, and within seconds, the ambulance pulled away. As it disappeared in the distance, Cindy began to cry softly, turning the bracelet Bobby had given her around and around with trembling fingers.

"Take it easy, Cindy," Jamee said, wiping the tears from her eyes. "It'll be all right."

"Cindy, why don't Jamee and I get you home. You've had a long night," Darcy suggested.

"But what's going to happen to Bobby?" Cindy asked.

"Me and Tarah will go to the hospital and check on him," Cooper chimed in. "We'll call you when we learn something."

"Okay," Cindy said.

As they drove home, Jamee gave Cindy her jacket and sat in the back seat with her.

"Thanks for helping me tonight. I'm so sorry I put you through this," Cindy said.

"Cindy, we're your friends," Jamee said. "This is what friends do for each other. Just remember what you did for me last year."

"I can't believe this happened," Cindy said, wiping her eyes. "All this time, I thought Bobby had changed. And I know this sounds stupid, but he really made me feel special. Nobody ever made me feel that way before."

"It doesn't sound stupid, Cindy," Darcy said. "But you've got to learn that you are special, whether you're with a guy or not. When you need someone else to make you feel good about yourself, you're going to get into trouble. It may sound like something off a corny TV show, but it's true. What you're looking for doesn't come from others; it comes from inside you."

Cindy wiped her eyes in silence.

At Cindy's apartment, all three girls got out of the car together. "Thanks again," Cindy said. "You two are the best."

Jamee and Darcy gave Cindy a hug, holding her for several minutes before letting her go. When they finally got ready to leave, all three girls had red, moist eyes.

As soon as they left, Cindy quietly snuck into the apartment, grabbed the cordless phone, and went to her room. Her mother's bedroom door was closed, and Cindy was careful not to disturb her. Silently, she took off her costume, put on pajamas, and crawled into bed, replaying the evening's events in her mind. She could not shake the image of Bobby's unconscious body from her thoughts. It haunted her like a recurring nightmare.

At 5:00 in the morning, the phone rang. Cindy answered it with trembling hands.

"Cindy," Jamee said, "we just heard from Cooper. He's still at the hospital with the Wallace family. He said things looked bad for a while but that Bobby's going to be all right. His family's going to put him in a drug rehab program."

"Thanks, Jamee." Cindy sighed with relief. "Thank you for everything," she said before hanging up the phone. Instantly, tears of relief poured from her eyes.

Seconds later, Cindy heard a knock at her bedroom door. "Who's calling you at five in the morning?" her mother asked, sounding annoyed.

"No one. It was a wrong number," Cindy replied, struggling to hide the emotion in her voice.

Her mother opened the door and came into the dark bedroom. "Cindy, who were you just talking to?"

"Why do you care?" Cindy said.

"I'm not leaving this room until you tell me what's going on," her mother demanded, sitting at the foot of the bed.

"Oh, so now you're suddenly gonna try and play Mom," Cindy answered bitterly. She wanted to talk to her, but she couldn't hide the anger she felt—anger at Bobby for lying to her, anger at Mom for ignoring her, anger at Raffie for betraying them both. "Just leave me alone. That's what you always do."

"I don't know why I even bother. You know, I bumped into Mrs. Davis last night, and all she did is tell me how much you want to talk to me. That old woman's got no sense. She should mind her own business instead of telling me how to raise my child. There ain't no talkin' to you," her mother yelled and walked towards the door.

"Mom . . ." Cindy turned towards her. She wanted to tell Mom everything that had happened, but she just could not say the words. The anger in her chest was like a net holding the words back. Still, she struggled against it. "Please. Don't leave," she said, tears filling the corners of her eyes.

Her mother stopped at the bedroom doorway and turned around. For a second, the apartment was completely quiet. Her mother stood motionless and silent in the dim glow coming from a streetlight. It would be dawn soon.

Cindy tried to hide her emotions, but she was unable to suppress the tears that had begun slipping from her eyes.

"What is it, baby?" her mother asked. "Why are you crying?"

Cindy looked directly at her mother. She didn't know where to begin, what words to say, or how to say them. But she couldn't hold back any longer.

"Mom, there's just too much," Cindy said. "I don't know how to tell you 'cause I know you won't wanna listen. But I'm not gonna lie. Not to you, myself, or anyone. Not anymore," she said.

"Why don't you start at the beginning," her mother said, sitting down on the bed next to her daughter. "I'm listening."

Cindy stared into her mother's eyes. They seemed very tired but sincere. It had been a long while since Cindy had seen such a look on her mother's face. Impulsively, Cindy grabbed her mother's hand and began to talk. First, she explained her relationship with Bobby and the Halloween party. Then she described how Bobby had hurt her wrist and tried to choke her, and how he had overdosed on drugs. She even mentioned how Mrs. Davis, Harold, and Jamee had tried to keep her away from Bobby. Her mother shook her head as Cindy recounted the details.

"What were you doin' with a boy like that? Can't you see he was no good for you?" her mother said.

Cindy rolled her eyes. Even though her mother meant well, Cindy could barely restrain her impulse to yell at her. She knew Mom was just as blind about Raffie as she had been about Bobby. The only difference, Cindy thought, was that Mom was still ignoring the truth.

"You are just like me, Mom," she said. "We are exactly the same." Faint light from the approaching dawn was beginning to illuminate the small bedroom.

"What are you saying?"

"Mom, I ignored the truth about Bobby because I was afraid. I didn't listen to my friends or to what my eyes were telling me because I didn't want to be alone. I wanted someone to love me, someone to care about me, someone to show me that I am special, you know? The whole time, he was lying to me and doing who knows what else," Cindy explained. "Raffie's just like Bobby, Mom. And you are just like me." Her mother's jaw hung open as Cindy spoke.

Her mother shook her head. "No!" she said, her voice quivering. "Raffie and I are diff—"

"No, you're not!" Cindy yelled. "I bet Bobby got his drugs from Raffie. What about the car, and all the money? What about the fact that I saw Raffie outside the high school the other day? What do you think he's been selling to get all that cash? Everyone in the neighborhood knows about Raffie, and so do you. You just don't want to admit it. Face it, Mom. He's been lying to you, and you are letting him get away with it by lying to yourself. The worst part about it is that we're suffering, Mom. Look at us. All we ever do is yell at each other. I don't wanna do that any more," Cindy said, her heart pounding.

Cindy's mother sat still, staring off towards the morning light for awhile.

"The other day Raffie asked me to hold a package for him while he's away. He wouldn't tell me what it was, but when I asked him about it, he got very upset," she said, tears in her eyes. "I kept telling myself it was a present, but I don't know, Cindy . . . I don't know what to believe. I just thought we'd get married, but now, I don't know."

"Do you still have the package?" Cindy asked excitedly.

Suddenly the phone rang, piercing the morning quiet. Cindy looked at the clock. It was 6:15. "Who could be calling this early?" she asked.

Mom answered the phone. "Hello? Raffie? What's wrong? The police station! Now? Who—"

Cindy knew immediately what was happening. The police had finally traced drugs to Raffie, and they had arrested him. She grabbed her mother's arm. "Hang up, Mom! Hang up!"

"Cindy, this is an emergency! Raffie's at the police station," she said. "He says he's been falsely accused of selling drugs. He wants me to get some money from his apartment and bail him out."

"Mom, don't help him. He's a liar. Please. Just hang up! He's no good!"

Cindy's mother leaned back and looked to the ceiling. "Lord give me strength," she said. "Hold on a minute, Raffie," she said into the phone and then turned towards her daughter. "Cindy, go to my room and look under my bed. Raffie's package is there." Cindy rushed into the room and retrieved a brown paper sack.

"Open the package," Mom directed.

Cindy ripped open the paper. Underneath was a layer of plastic and beneath that a white powdery substance that coated her sweaty finger. "Look!"

Cindy's mother examined the package without a word. She wiped her eyes several times. Then, taking a deep breath, she picked up the phone and spoke calmly. "Raffie, I ain't coming for you," she said. "Me and my daughter are staying here. Take care of yourself. It seems that's all you care about." Then she hung up the phone and dialed the police.

"I'm so sorry, baby," Mom said, her eyes swollen and bloodshot. She had just finished telling the police officer everything she knew about Raffie.

"Yes, Raphael Whitaker has been

under observation for months," the officer said, giving the package to his partner. "We decided to move last night because we had two other overdoses yesterday with the same symptoms. Between that and evidence from Officer Ortiz at Bluford, we had all we needed to take Whitaker and his dealers off the street for a long time," he said as he walked out the door.

Cindy turned at the name Ortiz. Pedro had been an undercover police officer, Cindy realized. She shook her head in disbelief.

"All this time, the truth was right in front of me, but I was blind," Mom said when the officer left, her voice cracking. "I've been a terrible mother. I've ignored you, I've hurt you. I've pushed you away. But baby, I love you, and I am so sorry. You are the most precious thing in my life, and I'm not gonna let no man get between us ever again."

For several minutes, the two embraced each other in silence. Cindy's mind raced with questions about the future, questions about their family and about Bobby, questions she could not answer. "What's gonna happen, Mom?" she finally asked.

"I don't know, baby. We got a lot to sort out. We don't have much money. It's gonna be hard," her mother said, blowing her nose.

Mom was right, Cindy thought. The future was uncertain, and they had much work to do. But looking at her mother in the bright morning sunshine, Cindy thought for once that the work was not impossible.

"I think things are gonna get better around here," Mom said. "I really do."

"I think so too, Mom."

Just then they heard a knock at the door.

"It's just me," a familiar voice said. "I knew y'all had a long night, and I thought you might like some breakfast." Cindy opened the door to see Mrs. Davis's wide smile greeting her. Harold stood behind her holding a large tray filled with eggs, bacon, and fried potatoes.

"Isn't it a glorious morning, child?" Mrs. Davis beamed.

"It sure is, Grandma Rose," Cindy said, welcoming the two neighbors into the apartment. "It sure is."

Find out what happens next at

BLUFORD HIGH

The Bully

A new life. A new school. A new bully. That's what Darrell Mercer faces when he and his mother move from Philadelphia to California. After spending months living in fear, Darrell is faced with a big decision. He can either keep running from this bully—or find some way to fight back.

Turn the page for a special sneak preview. . . .

With a cold November wind stabbing through his jacket, Darrell Mercer took one last walk with his best friend, Malik Stone.

"Man, I can't believe you're movin' to California tomorrow," Malik said. "I just can't believe I won't see you no more."

Darrell shook his head. He could not believe it either. In just a few hours, he would leave the only neighborhood he had ever known in his fifteen years. Soon his street, his school, and every friend he had in the world would be thousands of miles away. Thinking about what was ahead of him, Darrell felt like a man going to his own hanging.

"I'll miss you, man," Darrell said, his voice wavering.

The boys had known each other since first grade at Harrison School on 44th

Street. Their neighborhood was definitely not one of Philadelphia's best. Most of the buildings were old and decaying, and graffiti covered just about every one. Some houses were vacant, and a few had broken windows. Abandoned cars rusted along many streets, and occasionally local newscasts would run a story about city crime and feature this area as an example. To many people, the neighborhood was trouble, but to Darrell and his friends, it was home. True, there were guys selling drugs on street corners. But there were also good kids like Malik, Big Reggie, and Mark. Because of them, Darrell had never felt alone.

Inside the rundown homes that lined Darrell's block, there were always people to turn to in times of trouble. Across the street was old Mr. Corbitt, who sat on his porch each day and waved at everyone who passed by. And in the corner house was Mrs. Morton. She made sweet-potato pie for people in the neighborhood, especially Darrell and his mother.

"This'll help you grow," Mrs. Morton would say whenever she left a pie at their apartment. It never seemed to work, but Darrell didn't mind because the pies were delicious.

Darrell had always been short for his age. At fifteen years old, he was just under five feet. He was also skinny, without a respectable muscle in his small body. Back in September, Darrell had dreaded starting Franklin High, but his friends were right there with him. If anyone picked on Darrell during those first weeks of school, they had the other guys to deal with too. But all that was changing.

Darrell was moving to California two months after the school year had begun. It was the first day of high school all over again, only this time Darrell did not have his friends to protect him. Darrell did not admit it to anyone, but he was scared.

"Want a cheesesteak?" Malik asked when they came to Sal's Steaks.

"I guess," Darrell said. Sal made the best cheesesteaks in the neighborhood, or maybe in the entire city. They were loaded with gobs of dripping cheese and just the right amount of fried onions.

"This one's on me," Malik said, a crack in his voice. Physically, Malik was the opposite of Darrell. He was six feet tall with big muscular shoulders. Although he was just a freshman, Malik had already earned a position on the Franklin High School varsity football team. Ever since they were young boys, Darrell was thankful that he was Malik's friend because nobody messed with Malik or his friends. Watching Malik return with the steaks, Darrell felt a wave of sadness sweep over him.

"This is our last cheesesteak together," Malik said, handing one to Darrell.

"Thanks, Malik," Darrell said. Normally, he would devour the cheesesteak quickly, but now, for the first time he could remember, he felt as if he could not eat. His throat seemed to close up on him. *It isn't fair,* he thought. Why did things happen this way? Why did he have to leave his home and his best friends? And why, of all times, did it have to be in the middle of his first year of high school? He knew why. His mother had explained it many times, but she could not change how he felt. Realizing he would hurt Malik's feelings if he did not accept his gift, Darrell forced the cheesesteak down his throat. He knew it would be the last meal he would ever have with his friend.

The boys continued walking down the darkening street. Every storefront was painful for Darrell to see. He knew he would not be back to the old neighborhood again, at least not for a long time. He glanced across the street at the old grocery store. Today it looked warm and inviting, even though the owners charged too much for meats, and the fruits and vegetables were not always fresh. At the corner, they passed the laundromat where his mother did her wash. A black mechanical rocking horse stood next to the door so parents could entertain their children while waiting for the laundry to dry. Once, Darrell and Malik gave coins to a little neighborhood kid so he could ride.

"Remember when Rasheed took four rides on our money?" Darrell asked.

"Yeah," Malik said glumly.

It was dark now. Mom had asked Darrell to be home early. The bus was leaving at 5:15 the next morning.

Darrell looked down at the emerald-green shards of a shattered beer bottle glistening in the street light. "I guess I gotta go now, Malik," he said heavily. "I gotta go home."

Home. What a mockery that word was now, Darrell thought. Home was an empty apartment with boxes in the middle of the floor, packed for the move to California. Mrs. Morton was handling the shipping for them.

"You been a real brother to me," Darrell said. "I . . . I love you, man," Darrell blurted, his voice melting into embarrassing sobs.

Malik grabbed Darrell and gave him a bear hug. For a second, Darrell's face was jammed into Malik's shirt. Then the two separated, and, without a word, started walking in opposite directions. After a few steps, Darrell began to run.

"It's not fair!" he yelled, as he sprinted through the dark. He felt as if he were being robbed, that things were being taken from him that he could never replace.

Sure, Malik would miss him, Darrell thought, but Malik was big, and he had tons of friends. Darrell was sure Malik would be fine without him.

But Darrell was not so certain about his own future. The days ahead stretched out before him like a dark road filled with dangerous shadows. It would be like the summer Mom sent him to a camp for inner-city kids. The camp director promised Darrell and his mother that he would experience adventures in the out-doors away from the dangers of the city. What Darrell ended up experiencing was torment from a kid who wanted nothing more than to make anyone weaker than him feel as miserable as possible.

The kid's name was Jermaine, and his favorite activity was torturing Darrell. He pushed Darrell into the lake. He dropped worms into Darrell's ice cream. He put laxative in Darrell's pudding, making him sick for two days. During the whole time at camp, Darrell remained silent about Jermaine. What choice did he have? He knew he did not stand a chance against Jermaine in a fight, and he knew if he told one of the adults, Jermaine would retaliate the next time no one was watching. But the biggest reason Darrell never said anything to anyone was that he was ashamed of being so helpless. At least if he kept everything to himself, no one else would know how pathetic he was. Lately, whenever Darrell thought about California, he imagined some kid like Jermaine waiting for him. Or maybe several Jermaines. And nobody would be there to help him. Not Malik. Not anyone.

As Darrell walked down the alley towards his apartment, a stray cat greeted him. It purred and rubbed its face against his calf, looking up at him with radiant green eyes.

"This is it, Max," Darrell said, petting the cat's soft gray fur. "Your last pet from me. Goodbye, Max." The cat circled his legs.

Darrell and his mother had lived in the apartment for six years. Before that, they lived in a small house. Darrell's father was with them then, but he was killed in a car accident. After his death, Darrell's mother got a job as a clerk for an insurance agency, and they moved to the apartment.

For years, everything had been fine, but then in August a larger insurance company bought out the agency where Darrell's mother worked. To save money, the company eliminated her job along with hundreds of others. For a while, she tried to find work nearby that would pay her enough to support the two of them, but the only jobs she could find were in fast-food restaurants. Then in October, Darrell's Uncle Jason, her brother, called and offered her a job in California paying twice what she could make in their neighborhood. Darrell understood why his mother chose to take the job, but he did not like her decision. *I wish he never would have called,* Darrell thought as he walked up the steps to the apartment.